NOTHING PURPLE, NOTHING BLACK

NOTHING PURPLE, NOTHING BLACK

Paul Crawford

The Book Guild Ltd
Sussex, England

First published in Great Britain in 2002 by
The Book Guild Ltd
25 High Street
Lewes, East Sussex
BN7 2LU

Typesetting in Bembo by
SetSystems Ltd, Saffron Walden, Essex

Printed in Great Britain by
Antony Rowe Ltd, Chippenham, Wiltshire

A catalogue record for this book is
available from the British Library

ISBN 1 85776 574 5

100265095 6

For Rhiannon and Jamie
With special thanks to
Vernon Conway

1

Harvey jumped the remaining wave of steps and burst onto the platform, narrowly missing a pram. He spun round, apologising in flight, his swan-necked umbrella a crosier, his large garnet ring unnoticed by the cursing mother who struggled with her lot. For an instant, he recalled yesterday's headline in the paper, not of his fall from grace but simply his disappearance. But he knew that this was just mustard seed to the stories that might eventually be told. He pelted into the crowd, his black leather holdall catching legs as he went, the chill pulling steam from his lips, the canopied lights digging shadows beneath his gas-flame eyes.

Along the platform he wove his way, aware he was being followed, and stopped beneath yet another sign for Templeford Junction and glanced back. Whoever kept on his tail slipped out of sight. He convinced himself it was a journalist. Why didn't he leave him alone? All he wanted on this black, comfortless day was to be left in peace, left to mull over his decision and find some pattern to his life again. He reached the far end of the platform where the green canopy gave way to slicing rain, and determined to join the train at the last second, to escape, as in films, his shadow.

So he changed tack from flight to pretence. Settling into the last dry seat on the platform, he composed himself to appear at ease, though his damp trousers clung coldly to his skin and streaks of greying hair lay across his scalp like limp, dead fingers. In this manner he would wait. Then, just before the train nudged out from beneath the canopy into the wet, he would jump on board.

As he waited, tapping the silver tip of his umbrella against his shin, he looked out at the backs of the houses above the embankment. He paid particular attention to the last of these, huddled beside the iron bridge, only a few bricks showing between a plague of billboards. It was there that he had spent the night.

He had searched yet again for some bolt hole and, after walking soullessly back and forth along Templeford High Street, thought he was condemned to a windy shop alcove, until the discreet 'B&B' sign caught his flagging eye. The woman who answered the door seemed pleased to hear his refined voice, though somewhat unsure what it signified in the circumstances; for he had the look of a hunted man and his clothes that of an undertaker down on his luck. But she smelt money in the curl of his accent and showed him a room. It wasn't up to much: just a bed, side table, two-cup kettle and sachets of coffee in an ashtray. But it felt homely in the strange way a bare room in a seminary can, the emptiness a decoration in itself; and it had a burning radiator over which he draped his rinsed purple socks.

On the morning, the landlady took twenty pounds from him and bid him good day, but not without passing comment on his ring.

'That's fancy,' she said, but with an undertow of suspicion in her voice.

'Like a bishop's,' answered Harvey, baring his chest.

For a moment, the comment had held some power over the woman, bringing a frown to her brow as she studied him more closely: the stubble, red fleshy cheeks, prematurely grey hair, wise eyelids, vague dimples. Then she laughed.

'Go on with you,' she cajoled, showing him into the vestibule. 'Bishops are old.'

His eyes fell back down through the rain to his feet and the tapping umbrella, and Harvey guessed the reporter had sent a side-kick to the B&B by now, to frisk the landlady for gossip, to steal into the room and put a hand into the waste-paper basket, like a child's into a lucky dip. Keeping his head facing the glass of a carriage, Harvey rolled his eyes to the right, trying to catch his shadow off guard. But again, nothing. For the first time, it entered his mind that he might be paranoid. He pinched his lip between his teeth and wondered when the train would start rolling. He had to get the timing just right.

The announcer spoke: 'The train now standing at platform five is the fourteen-fifty for London Euston.'

Harvey looked at his gold watch, shivered a little and wondered whether London was a good idea after all. Travelling without paying the fare was tricky. But he had few options. If he reached London, he could rest up with Montgomery in Kingston, brace himself for the new life he was to lead, not have to explain himself. Montgomery wouldn't care a damn if the Pope himself took to the spare bed, so long as he didn't moralise about his girlfriends. And surely Montgomery would lend him some money to get by, at least for a while.

Good old Montgomery and his *unnatural appetencies*, as Bishop Fowler called them, who found him masturbating in the 'Lavatorium'. 'I hope that's your nose you're rubbing,' he had told him. But the sudden interruption made Montgomery grip himself so fiercely that when his insides exploded a little bit of mistletoe jumped the toilet door and landed in the bishop's hair. That was that. Out he went. Montgomery told everyone the story down the years. He was proud of the athleticism of his seed. 'It would run up a drainpipe,' he argued, but had never produced a child from it. Unlike Montgomery, Harvey stayed the course and eventually went to the American College in Louvain and the English College in Rome. They had him down for big things, and he was

3

ready and willing. He had *unnatural appetencies* like everyone else, but he was better at public relations. At least, until recently.

Harvey looked at his watch again, at the train, and along the platform to see if the reporter was still there. He wondered if he should seek out Montgomery. He hadn't seen him for years, of course, but that didn't matter. He was one of very few people that he felt would understand his predicament. He had thought of going south-west to the nuns at Baddersley, or to the monks on Caldey Island. The latter had seemed attractive. He felt the Abbey's boat roll from side to side as it hit the currents off Tenby Bay and chug alongside the sandy beach before heading out to the island with its lighthouse, monastery and village, and at night, its ghosts. And it was the island of love after all. It was where he had met Olwyn. Olwyn, whom he had depended on, and who had now gone from his life. But Harvey slowly put such ideas out of his mind. He couldn't face running to fellow priests, nuns or monks, not now, not after what had happened. Maybe some of them would be helpful, but he couldn't do it. He had to get away. He had to go all the way down the snake and start again somehow. But how and where he just did not have a clue.

He felt terribly vulnerable, and fear took his neck more tightly than a Roman collar. He wanted to pray, but it was as if he no longer knew what that meant. With no footholds, and knowing only poverty and loneliness, he looked upon the future as if it were a big gun pointing back at him. Deep down, he hoped he would see Olwyn again. But everything had become so difficult and clouded. How could he go to her? How could he heap scandal onto scandal? He knew that for the time being, it was best to keep clear, best to leave the dust to settle.

Harvey sensed that he didn't qualify for life anymore. What would anyone want with him? He was useless to everyone except reporters, who sensed he had let the show down big-time and were on the scent. He hung his confused head. He had to do something, go somewhere. He needed to hide for a while, get a little job doing God knows what. He knew that most priests who leave go into some sort of caring work, but he couldn't work in a hospital if his life depended on it. He had hated his time as hospital chaplain – with the dead all day. The thought made him shiver. Social work would be better, however, and there was more money in it.

But whatever course he took, Montgomery would be a useful first stepping stone into society, he decided, staring vacantly at his umbrella: he was a shade between the cathedral and the brothel. And while he stayed in London he might find work and get a room and spend some of his first wages on some new clothes – nothing purple, nothing black. Just normal, everyday gear. Of course, he wouldn't shake off any lingering conservatism overnight. He wouldn't find shapelessness quite that easily. It would take time. And time was something he had plenty of. But within this time, he saw failure and rejection. What else could be his lot? He had met so many priests who had left the ministry. He had seen the hardness of heart that met them. And often, like himself, they left penni-less, with no stipend or pension to live on. Worse than this, he could not forget those who had killed themselves.

Harvey wished he had saved a little money along the way, since what he had would not last long. Perhaps he should have dipped into the collection plate. But theft was not in him. Well, almost.

He checked his watch again and willed the fingers on. Other passengers had the same idea, looking at the old station clock, willing its fingers to bend round the white face. He wanted to go, but the whistle was nowhere near the guard's lips and the doors of the train gaped open. They would have to be shut. Harvey rummaged in his pocket and brought out the letter he had received from the Archbishop. Only too aware of its contents, he opened it out. He laughed with no heart through his nostrils and shook his head. Who wouldn't? He shook his head at the words of condemnation.

He read the letter twice more before sticking it back in his pocket. Why had he taken the office? He had gone ahead without considering how destructive it would be in the end, how hopeless it would make Olwyn. God, how wrongly he had read the situation. How selfish his needs. He should have declared *nolo episcopari*. But no, he had put on the purple cassock and skullcap. He had let the mitre sit up on that silly, silvery head of his. He had let them make him the youngest, and now shortest-serving bishop in England. He could have left unspectacularly. He could have evaporated like so many before him. He could have become one of the many priests who had left the Church since *Vatican II*, or *the sequel* as Harvey called it. He could have been scandal-free. But he allowed himself to be polished, exalted, preferred, given height from which to tumble down.

After pinching his eyes dry, he wrung his hands and looked along the platform again. This time he saw the reporter, who had grown complacent watching Harvey's stooped rigidity. He stood by the restaurant, nonchalantly thumbing his way through a broadsheet. There was something quite ugly about the man. But Harvey barely had the chance to grasp his repulsive pockmarked face when he disappeared into the restaurant. Now was his chance, Harvey realised, seeing the guard's signal that the train was ready to depart.

On the neighbouring bench, Roland Crystal watched the dark, hunched figure of Harvey look round like a hunted animal, eyes too piercing to be just looking. This was just how he needed his victims to be. The more anxious the better. He had studied his prey closely and decided that he would be perfect.

6

Crystal could commit his crime easily; a crime no judge could pass sentence on, any prison could punish. Over the years he had found Templeford Junction convenient for his time-wasting, the progress of which kept him alive. Licking his finger and thumb, he snuffed the Park Drive he had scrounged from Molly at the newspaper stall, and saved it for later, pushing it behind his blackened ear. Then, dabbing his tongue at the blister on his lip, he set his eyes to his prey. What Crystal thought of as a young-old man stood now, clasping his umbrella as if wringing rain from its fabric and looking down the platform as if someone was after him. Crystal smiled weirdly. Ripe for the picking, he thought. If he wasn't mistaken, a mask of sweat had caught his victim's silver-topped brow, had given him an unreal luminescence beneath the canopy lights. Crystal hitched up his oilskin trousers and left the bench. He hadn't lost any of his sense of timing.

His prey, looking now from the potent, hanging train to the restaurant, lifted his holdall from the ground and stood with the posture of imminent flight, his umbrella horizontal, like a baton. The old stock train doors were closed now. The train lurched forward suddenly and froze, with the illusion that it wasn't moving at all, but it was. Crystal saw Harvey rush forward in a panic. The train stopped again. Someone was shouting out further down the station. It was the guard telling Harvey to hurry up and get on board. Crystal was off his mark like a shot, despite his cumbrous oilskins. He needed to be. His quarry had an agility that belied his grey hair.

Harvey's hand fell on the door handle and began to cork-screw when Crystal pulled at his elbow. Harvey looked round and into the harsh, raw face of the stranger. This was no reporter. This guy was like a boxer, a fisherman, a tramp rolled into one. Crystal held onto Harvey's sleeve.

'I think you've lost something,' he said into his victim's perplexed eyes.

Harvey shook his head, and then glanced quickly towards the restaurant for fear that the reporter had witnessed his flight and might board the train further down.

'I don't think so,' snapped Harvey imperiously, turning his attention to opening the door. He could see the guard itching to get things underway. A terrible urgency gripped him, made this stranger's interruption painful.

Crystal looked on, keeping a firm grip of his prey's arm, feeling a rush of satisfaction as Harvey's features took on a tortured, desperate look. He could see time itself tearing into him and making him squirm on a hook, as already a rumour of movement passed from the handle of the train and begged decisiveness. The train halted once more. Harvey gritted his teeth and struggled, his umbrella and holdall in one hand, the train's bone-shaped handle in the other.

'I believe it's valuable,' added Crystal, his voice loud, forceful.

Reluctantly, Harvey turned from the inquisitive faces of passengers already on board and in their seats, and dropped his bag to the ground. It was no use struggling. Crystal's fingers had dug trenches around his elbow. Harvey knew that he could not physically separate himself.

'I don't know who you are,' he shouted, tears welling up as he looked for help from other people. 'But I have to catch this train.' Still Crystal held him firm, like a bully, his green eyes staring down, twitching with a perverse delight.

'Look, is this a mugging or what?' Harvey was perplexed, stumbling now, as the train looked ready to go. The guard kept putting his whistle to his lip and dropping it. Harvey knew that the automatic lock would come on soon, if it had not done so already.

Crystal did not answer. He looked at Harvey's quivering lip, tear-rimmed eyelids, flushed brow, and felt the trembling of his victim's arm as if it, not the wires above, carried electricity.

Like corpses, Harvey's words lay down on his tongue. Quickly he rummaged through his pockets with his free hand. He intended only a symbolic search.

'No, no,' he announced, playing light. 'Everything's here. Nothing missing. Now if you just let me get on my way, I won't say anything more about it.' He smiled falsely and made to pick up his umbrella and holdall, but Crystal held him back. The guard was shouting at them to stand clear. Overwhelmed, Harvey looked from stranger to train and back again, time running out. Crystal absorbed the anguish of the moment: the confusion, the disbelief, the torture.

'I have everything,' Harvey was shouting now, Crystal just a blur, a dark bruise behind streaming tears. 'Let go of me.'

The guard blew his whistle a final time, exasperated. Harvey felt that at any second the train would turn a breeze along the platform.

'I told you I have lost nothing. Now let me go!'

'Are you sure?' said Crystal, a lump in his throat, a tear tracking down his left cheek, and then soon after, down his right. 'Can't you feel it slipping away? Even now, surely . . . between the fingers . . . acid drops of wasted time . . . lost forever, never to be replaced? Gone. Don't you feel the pain? The sting? The loss?'

'What the bloody hell? No!' gasped Harvey, trying fruitlessly to break free.

But he did feel an arterial bleeding of time. He tried to cut the ravings of the man from his mind, but the words hit like the punctuation of rain as it began to tap against the canopy above Templeford Junction. And when his eyes cleared a little, it was to see the train flick its tail through the maw of tunnel. Then he felt wounded, bloodlessly, something – time – surgically removed.

'Ah,' sighed Crystal, 'you have helped so much.'

Incredulous, Harvey looked at the face of Crystal with its slug tracks of drying tears. Now he saw an expression of remorse. Crystal's grip relaxed and his fierceness evaporated, leaving his huge frame as pathetic as a scarecrow's after a storm. But Harvey had little sympathy. Despite his years of pastoral work as chaplain to a mental hospital, he wanted to smash his fist into Crystal's face. Harvey knew he must be a mental patient: filthy hair, unshaven chin, ill-fitting, strange clothing, and equally bizarre behaviour.

But Harvey was wrong. Crystal was no patient. At least not now that England's mental institutions had been boarded up, sold off or demolished. The mad and the sane shared the same bathwater of life these days. They shared the community. Besides, who could pretend that madness, even Crystal's own peculiar brand, could be contained? No, his madness had no boundaries. Walls would not keep it in – never could. And, like rain, it had its seasons.

Harvey felt little compassion for the time waster. There was a priest in him still, a bishop even. But these were desperate days for Harvey. And he felt little desire, if he had ever had it, to be saintly. He really wanted to hit out at the man who had postponed his journey south, but Crystal was big and the memory of his grip warned Harvey to keep calm. Now, with the train gone, he didn't know what to do. He would have to wait for the next one. Crystal did not move away. He stood too close to look natural, as if he had just broken from giving Bishop Harvey a passionate kiss.

Harvey reached down and picked up his umbrella and holdall and knocked the dust off them. Crystal wiped his eyes and stepped back, looking gormless, as if he had just woken up. He seemed to take stock, then dabbed his blistered lip with his tongue, and for his size appeared decidedly sheepish. Harvey looked at the departure board and saw that there was not even a time for the next train to London. He placed the umbrella between the handles of his bag and with his free hand pinched his lips into an exasperated beak. He wondered whether he would ever escape Southwick.

In the last two days he had put just sixty miles between himself and the parish at Hickley. It was as if he had glue on the soles of his feet. And now this mental patient came from nowhere and stole his journey. Still bemused by it all, he walked along the edge of the platform, keeping an eye out for the reporter who, he was sure, still haunted the restaurant. But there were lots of people looking out. Whoever it was, good luck to him, thought Harvey. The press wanted a story, of course. They wanted sauce on it. He laughed down his nose. There was plenty of sauce to be had.

Crystal moved alongside Harvey, opening his mouth several times as if about to speak, his oilskins gleaming away. Harvey stopped, with the pit and track behind him. He was facing the disabled toilet. Not far away were the stairs which he had descended not long ago. Beyond the hood of canopy the rain was falling hard again. Crystal watched him closely. He had done his deed, whatever that was. Harvey was sure the poor man had little choice over the matter, yet couldn't give a cardinal's fart for him. Crystal took a nub from behind his ear and lit up, striking what looked like his last match. Thumbing the damp, grubby matchbox into his breast pocket, he hitched his trousers, and tightened the string about his waist.

'I'm sorry about what I did to you,' Crystal told him. 'It's just something I have to do.'

Harvey had guessed as much already. But he didn't expect to see a big smile from Crystal, which came against the grain. It wasn't a normal smile. There was something missing. His teeth, like yellow corn, were poor ambassadors.

Harvey flexed his arm, testing his elbow, wondering if

11

bruises might show where the stranger had gripped him. He cursed under his breath and moved further away. But Crystal insisted on following him along the white line, his brown-necked fingers sticking the foul nub to his lip, always resting against the small, dark bubble of skin.

'Again, I am sorry if I hurt you in any way,' he said. 'I don't mean any harm. You see, well, only I have to do it. Or else. . . .' There was a long pause when the stranger's thoughts seemed blocked. Then he continued. 'My name's Crystal, by the way. And you?' A puff of smoke stroked his cheek.

Harvey looked down at Crystal's shorn-off gumboots and shook his head. He did not know what to say. He glanced up into the stranger's eyes and stubbly chin.

'You don't want to know my name,' he told him. 'I'm not likely to. . . .' But Harvey stopped himself. The poor chap was mental, he reminded himself.

'Jesus,' he muttered under his breath. 'I'm Harvey,' he told him.

'Harvey,' Crystal repeated. 'Harvey. Now Harvey, you were in part to blame for all that, you know . . . business back there. If you hadn't been so anxious, so desperate to catch that train, I would have left you alone. None of this would have happened. Do you see?'

'Not at all, but I'll take your word for it.'

Harvey began to seriously consider a spell in the disabled toilet. But he just picked up the pace and tried to put some platform between him and Crystal.

'I couldn't help thinking you were on the run or something,' began Crystal, taking a draw. 'You seem so jumpy.' The smoke unfurled with his slow, methodical words. 'Am I right? Some-one after you? You don't have to say. Where is he? Over there? You keep looking that way.'

Harvey did not answer.

'The law?'

12

'No, nothing like that,' said Harvey, half listening, half dreaming, looking about distractedly.

'A detective then? Marital problems? Wife, you know . . .' Crystal flicked the nub onto the track and licked his blister.

'Wife?' Harvey afforded a laugh. A cynical laugh of a man who had always compromised himself in that department.

'Loan shark then? Or are you being hunted by those who are hunting me?'

Crystal looked back over his shoulder as he said this. Harvey just shook his head at the stranger's persistence.

'You don't live in London, do you?'

'I might,' said Harvey.

'No. I can tell. You're homeless. The grime on your collar,' he said. 'Dead giveaway. Now that's a funny-looking shirt.' He could see the two slots that had held the missing clerical band.

Harvey was in the doldrums now, unable to shift one way or the other. He winced at the idea of being homeless. It stung him to think that he was closer to being in this stranger's predicament than he wanted to admit.

Harvey had no family to fall back on. His father and mother were dead and offered him nothing but momentary warmth when he remembered them in the little house in Ardinweald. Like well-pulled teeth, they had left nothing behind, not even a vacant property, nothing but the knowledge that should he fall, no one would be there to catch him. He saw his mother's proud blue eyes at the ordination ceremony. Her black wiry hair stood thin on the crown of her head. She had done her best to cover her bald patches. She was holding out a gold watch she had bought, the one he now wore. Then, a few days later, she had died. His father caught her elbow as it were, and tumbled with her into a double grave. And the words of Kilgarriff stuck in his throat this day in Templeford as they had done at his consecration as bishop: 'Your family must be so proud of you.' What family? He had no family. Not even a dog or cat. Kilgarriff, who had recommended his appointment as bishop, knew nothing of Harvey's absent family. The frail rag of memory that was his mother – a thickly powdered orange face – lost its edges and began to fade. Other things were on his mind as well. He began to look at the stairs which rose steeply to the exit, and wanted to shake off that reporter.

'Do you need a place to stay? I've got a place,' Crystal told him.

Harvey knew that there was little money left in his pocket, that there was almost nothing between him and the gutter. But he did not find the idea of sharing a roof with a mentally ill person attractive. He had quite accurate visions of run-down hostel accommodation. And although his experience told him that the mad were usually harmless compared to the sane, he did not want to try his luck. He was down and out, maybe, but not desperate. At least he tried to convince himself about this. Besides, Montgomery would bail him out. If he was there. If Harvey got there. The ashes of his former cotton-wool life stirred.

'No thank you,' he told Crystal. 'I've got to get along now.'

He had broken away from the white line and walked towards the stairs, to the right of the paper stall. Crystal tagged along behind, thumbs hitched into his buttonholes, duffel bag swinging to and fro on his wide, greasy back.

No sooner had Harvey drawn alongside the news-crammed paper stall, when he caught sight of the reporter who had followed his every move. He was standing bold as brass halfway up the iron and wood stairwell. It was him all right. He stood smiling widely, camera hanging from its strap. Harvey jerked away, flinching, pushing against Crystal, who stood in his way.

'That him?' Crystal asked, catching Harvey in his big palms.

The journalist was lifting his camera, and a series of blue flashes burnt the air, lighting up his own gaunt, pock-marked face. When Harvey removed his hand from his brow and blinked a softer light into his eyes, the paper man had disappeared through the turnstile. Harvey was dazed. He stumbled towards the newspaper stand, with Crystal at his back. As he did so, Molly recognised him: 'You're that bishop!' she shouted and began to thumb the *Evening Post* with her red, scoured fingers.

'He's that bishop!' she cried again, at Crystal this time, barely keeping her pipe between her lips. 'The one what's run off!' Molly rolled up the paper, trying to gain Crystal's attention. Harvey's printed face blurred as she waved the makeshift totem in the air. But Crystal was off on the heels of the bishop, who had about-turned and was climbing the stairs into the dying light.

Driven by some untold need, Crystal followed Harvey out of the station and into the backstreets of Templeford. Here the hounding began. And it was a hounding. All across town, in and out of shops, down alleyways, across the churchyard, and amid the detritus of the old open-air market place, Crystal followed Harvey. Now and again, Harvey stopped, swore at him, and told him to leave him alone. That's all he wanted – to be left alone. But Crystal did not turn round and saunter off. He kept up with him. He shouted to him that he could help, that he was sorry he had made him miss his train, and that there was plenty of room in his hostel just outside town. And unless he had money to burn, it would be better than a night on the street.

'You can stay at the hostel,' offered Crystal, coming closer.

Harvey broke his thoughts and frowned.

'It's dry enough, warm even.'

But Harvey brushed him aside and for the next few hours walked himself to exhaustion around the streets of Templeford. His poverty added to his general exhaustion and frustration. What money he had wouldn't take much burning. He didn't know where to go next. Eventually, he slumped down in a desperate, pathetic heap against a wall and covered his silver-moon head with both hands. He stayed like this for some time before parting his fingers and looking out across the street. On the other side, Crystal looked back at him, a cigarette bleeding out of the darkness of his face, the light from the street lamp in his eyes. Harvey groaned weakly and shook his head. If someone had bent close to his cold mouth, they would have heard a word he had tied up with palm leaves all his life. The barest 'Fuck' left his lips like the break of a saliva bubble.

At long last, incapable of protesting anymore or providing for himself a better opportunity, Harvey gave in to Crystal and accepted the invitation, bizarre as it was, to stay at the hostel. He told himself that he must be crazy to accept such an offer. But he had no fight to work his way back to the station and catch a train to London. Besides, what if the railway police caught him dodging his fare? Hadn't he been humiliated enough without a night in a cell? And even if he managed to get away without paying his fare, what if Montgomery had moved? What then?

Harvey did not much fancy walking the streets of London. He was tired and hungry. And it was getting late. If he sheltered for the night and got some rest, he would be better off, he decided. Perhaps, he could sell his ring or pectoral cross the next day, and then travel onwards. By now the dark had spirited away St Agatha's, and left him looking at the homeless of Templeford shifting about on the litter-strewn cobbles, and heading off for poor night cover beneath the market traders' awnings.

2

'Don't get me wrong, but you look nothing like a bishop,' said Crystal, making a snowball of loose newspaper and placing it along with several others in the grate. It was bitterly cold, and Harvey sat close to the unlit grate in expectation, rubbing his hands together and blowing warm air up over his nose. He watched as Crystal scouted for a live match, widening his eyes to draw the poor light that crept into the hostel room. Outside, the run-down estate on the outskirts of Templeford looked hostile.

'I try to last as long as I can without putting the light on,' Crystal explained. 'Otherwise, her downstairs has a go.'

Harvey shrugged, doubting his good sense in agreeing to bed down in this place, with its strange hops-like smell. And more, he found it difficult to fathom what he had let himself in for by leaving the security of the Church behind him. He had moved from a closed world into a frighteningly open one. He had begun a social descent. He felt distant from himself. Here he was, miles from his old parish, stinking, poor and cold. And sharing company with a stranger who had assaulted him. But at least the accommodation was free.

'Fancy, a bishop staying with me,' Crystal went on, striking a match and waving it gently at the paper. Harvey said nothing. He tried to sit more comfortably on the little stool that Crystal had handed him and let the awkwardness of his situation melt a little in the yellow flames.

Crystal looked leaner now without his oilskins. They lay where he had thrown them, spread out like a huge bat on the cushionless sofa. He took a fistful of wood from a tin bucket beside the fire and sprinkled it onto the shrinking paper balls. Harvey reached into his pocket again and took out Kilgarriff's letter. He read it through one more time before throwing it into the grate. The thing shrunk to nothing, but not before Crystal read the last few lines.

And all that time you were up to your weather-house tricks, dragging Christ Himself through the mud, and bringing shame on me.

With regret,

+ James Kilgarriff, Archbishop of Southwick

Crystal wanted to ask how Harvey had found himself down on his luck in Templeford, of all places East Vale, but resisted. What was all that business about 'weather-house tricks'? He wanted to ask him, but few guests had ever found their way into Crystal's room, and he liked company and wanted to keep it. He had spent so many dark winter nights as lonely as hell, that he did not want to offend Harvey any more than he had done already by stopping him getting his train. He hoped Harvey didn't think he was a brute for what he did. He wondered if he should apologise again, but kept silent. Harvey must understand, he decided. After all, he was here. He was keeping him company.

'It's warming up in here,' he said. Harvey agreed, rubbing his hands and trying to smile. The fire glinted from his ring and gold watch. He pulled the flaps of his longcoat over his knees.

'At least it's dry,' Harvey said, watching Crystal get up and go over to a cubbyhole.

'Tea?' Crystal shouted back, a blue glow emanating from a

hidden bedsit cooker. From outside the room, down the hallway, a toilet flushed somewhere.

'Please, that would be nice,' answered Harvey, sniffing and stretching his palms like a blessing over the fire.

How coldly the gold pectoral cross lay beneath his shirt. It hung like an icicle against his breastbone. How far he had fallen. How far from home, wherever home was. He had always been homeless at home. But still, a night-light of hope held him together. He kept his nerve. I am all right, he told himself. Things can only get better. Of course, he felt bad about taking things that did not rightly belong to him. Like a devious goldsmith rubbing gold dust in his hair to wash out later, Harvey had taken with him his ring of office and cross and chain. He had even taken away the gold-laced mitre which lay in his holdall like some magician's accessory. But what choice did he have? They were his only assets. Yet, as if confirming his guilt, he felt a phantom pressure on his skull where the mitre had sat.

While Crystal made tea, Harvey began to have one of his panic attacks. It had happened several times since leaving the ministry and joining the big wide world. It was worst in brightly lit shops and crowds. His heart thumped out of rhythm in his chest and his palms bled sweat. He fought the feeling, standing up and pacing round. I am a stone, he told himself. I am a stone and refuse to break up. The thought kept back the panic. He held it down, swallowed at the nausea, and gradually his heart settled again.

'Here,' said Crystal, handing him a steaming mug of tea, sacrificing his fingers to the hot rim so as to let Harvey grip the handle. Harvey thanked him and sat back down on his stool. Crystal placed his mug on the mantelpiece and rummaged through his pockets for a nub, eventually finding a lipsticked roach. He lit it, took his tea, and perching on the edge of the sofa, kicked off his gumboots.

'So, what do you think of the old place, eh?' he asked, enjoying his nub. 'Not bad? Fit for a bishop?'

'Forget the bishop lark. I'm just Harvey now. Call me Harvey.'

'You still look, well, priestly.'

Harvey looked at his clothes and nodded.

'I suppose I do.' Then he wondered at his host's name. 'It is Crystal isn't it?'

'Roland's my first name. But never call me that. I prefer Crystal.'

A silence followed and both Harvey and Crystal happily moved into it, not unproductively. They glanced at each other from time to time, trying to delve beneath the skin of outward appearances. But Crystal didn't like too much eye contact. He avoided it. And Harvey did not eyeball him. He sensed Crystal's discomfort with eyes. Harvey wanted to ask him about his strange behaviour at the station. But he thought better of it. He did not know this man. He did not know whether he could trust him. Certainly, he wasn't all there.

'I have a head problem,' said Crystal after a little while. 'I guess you know that.'

'We're all a little strange,' said Harvey. 'Any of us – if you look closely. Not all there, you know.'

Harvey let his eyes gaze into his tea.

'It's kind of you to say that,' said Crystal. 'Roland Crystal is more than a diagnosis.' He sucked heavily on his nub, wedged as tightly as ever against the blister on his lip.

Harvey had met hundreds of mentally ill people during his years of ministry. He had taken them in, fed them, listened to their ramblings. And now it seemed kind of ironic to be taken in by Crystal. Harvey looked out of the window at the clear, cold sky, and over the buildings of East Vale. From here, towards the west, lay Templeford's white lights. The words of Crystal slipped away.

Harvey thought of his mother. A ghostly umbilical cord stretched out from him to her. She was always falling into his mind. She who resembled him so little, always on the tip of his brain like a growth. Maternal intrusions came, soft and voiceless. She had constructed his need for her over the years. Mother addiction did not come overnight. And Harvey sensed that this addiction had taken him into the priesthood. From his earliest days, his mother had set him on his knees, placed prayer cards into his hands. He had been dolled up as an altarboy. He had been sent to Holtham College, a Catholic boarding school. It was as if Harvey finally became a priest, not to serve God, but to serve his mother.

Now he tried to picture her, force more detail into his memory of her. It was difficult. Whenever detail emerged, so did a finger that swirled the pool of chemicals in his head. Clenched eyelids did not help. He would gain that narrow brow and those rosary bead eyes, then lose them. The false teeth would burn for a second and vanish; then her dry, polished nose and rheumatoid knuckles. He would see her standing next to his father in his sepia suit in the wedding photograph with dimple pits in her cheeks more formidable than his own. But however much he tried, memory gradually crumbled. Like patches of skin, unable to be drawn together and sewn up, the image of the woman who brought him into the world fell apart into breasts dimly remembered, barely sucked, and bikini coverings where brain-light streamed. There had always been too many absences of the mother that assured his desire for her. Wasn't it his lack of knowledge of her that bound him to her? Had she known this was the case? How much of herself had she deliberately hidden from him to make him endlessly search for her, endlessly desire her, even to the point of becoming what she wanted him to be: a priest?

His mother had handed out only tiny facts, emotions, stories of herself. The mother's art, to make herself the end-point, the place of completion for her son. She made him want to sit again on the womb-throne. But completion never came. She died painfully. Was that when the priesthood seemed just so much cock and bull? And when she slipped away like the sun behind a cloud, did he foolishly become a bishop in the hope of pleasing her? The ultimate gift for a dead Catholic mother.

It was some time before Harvey came back from the space beyond the window and looked down at his tea, the dregs evidence that, despite his trance, he hadn't wasted it. He looked across at Crystal.

'I didn't want to disturb you,' said Crystal. The light was on now, and he had drawn a mattress over to the other side of the room and covered it with several blankets taken from a cardboard box behind the sofa. 'I thought you'd be glad of some rest. I know it's early. But with no television, and it being winter, I usually kip down about seven although I don't sleep very well.' Then saying this, he dragged the mattress into a corner, leaving it less exposed, and as far as he considered, more comforting. For even though Harvey had been just one of his many victims, he couldn't help but feel for him, dislocated as he was from his previous life – a life which though mysterious seemed to reverberate with his own – both of them being outcasts.

Harvey placed the cup on the floor, suddenly aware that the fire in the grate was dying. He crossed the room.

'I haven't a clue what I'm doing here,' he said honestly, embarrassed, scratching the grey hair across his scalp and the slowly lengthening stubble on his chin. It was as if he had been boozing all day and suddenly woken in a stranger's bedroom. 'It's ridiculous. I just can't believe what has happened to me. I feel so, so – '

'Lost?'

'Yes, lost. But I'm starting to get used to it. Soon I'll ignore the feeling, like the starving do when flies walk all over their eyes.'

Harvey stood stranded on the small rectangle of threadbare carpet.

'Get some rest,' Crystal advised, pointing to the mattress tucked away in the corner.

'Thanks. I'll shut up. I'm rambling.'

'That's okay. Carry on, I don't mind. I've got all my life to listen to you. Nothing else is going on. Talk right through till tomorrow. Tell you what, talk right through forever.'

'Tomorrow,' Harvey mumbled to himself. 'What'll I do tomorrow. Go to London? Sell this first?' He tapped the face of his watch. 'Or this?' He pulled at his chain of office. 'Sell these and buy some clothes. Normal clothes. Nothing purple, nothing black.' The tips of his fingers were disturbing the little money left in his pocket. It was as light and misleading as a bus ticket.

Harvey's mind was rolling. He just couldn't believe that he was sharing digs with Crystal. And in Templeford, where nothing happened, where people did nothing, and where he would do nothing if he stayed. He shut his lips tight and resolved to let everything float for now. Sleep and forget what might or might not happen. Crystal farted. Harvey did not smile. The glow from Crystal's nub seemed to brighten momentarily.

Harvey crawled fully dressed beneath the few blankets that Crystal had dumped on top of the bare mattress. The flames from the grate did little to make the bed look inviting. It felt damp. Harvey rested his cheek on his arm and watched as Crystal finished his smoke, farted twice more, and turned over on the sofa. Adjusting the oilskins that covered him, Crystal succeeded in fanning his stink towards Harvey, who cupped his mouth and nose.

Soon enough, despite his professed insomnia, Crystal's throat was bubbling and snoring, but Harvey lay wide awake, facing a stark empty night. The initial relief on leaving his parish had gone. He wondered whether he should have stayed and braved things out. Yet he had felt so caught out that he reacted instinctively and ran, stopping only to throw a few things into his holdall. He had given no explanation. He had thought only of himself. In a fit of self-preservation he cut himself off from the person closest to him. And now surely he could not wind the clock back. Now he was left with a loneliness sprung from the arms of joy. It was bitter and frightened him. He succumbed to it and cried – not for the first time, and certainly not for the last.

Like Crystal, Harvey moved in and out of sleep all night. He twisted and turned on the damp mattress, trying fruitlessly to get comfortable. Each futile effort brought him to lying on his back, hands behind his head, and staring into the darkness. In a lull between Crystal's snoring, he heard the hiss of a car, and when that had gone, the blood thumping his own ears. He tried to think of nice, happy things. He thought of those ample breasts cupped so recently in the palms of his hands. But no sooner had these thoughts warmed him than they were chilled by the way everything had ended.

'Oh Jesus!' he cried out as he went through it all again, shuddering. There was an awful afterburn of shame imprinted on his mind. He couldn't blink it away. Hadn't he been a coward, spineless even? Hadn't he promised her a life he couldn't deliver? Now he was lying at the bottom of a self-made pit, looking up but incapable of moving, paralysed. As the night trickled away, so did large blebs of water from his eyes, constantly birthing, and rolling down into the shells of his ears.

3

Jim Kilgarriff wasn't laughing. Barry Tourville's joke froze in the air between them and fell silently onto the brash red carpet, across which the Archbishop paced, indentations from his impeccably polished shoes filling up like wet sand. He pulled at the cigarette between his erect, swearing fingers, letting the smoke trickle back like incense along his square jaw. It wasn't a time for jokes. He stood at the windows, gazing down the floodlit, slanting lawn to the blue-tiled swimming pool with its rain-puckered surface.

'Who would have thought that he could be so unprincipled, so Janus-faced? Why didn't he come and talk it out? But no, walking out like that. The press are loving every minute of it. The rubbish they're printing isn't doing us any good at all. Me, it isn't doing me any good. And what the hell is he going to do with himself now that he's made the big descent? Tell me that!'

'He'll come crawling back.'

'Oh, you think so, do you, Barry? Well, there's a bright side.'

'Wait and see,' Tourville told him. Kilgarriff shook his head, winced, and shook his head once more.

'No, I don't think so. That's not Harvey, is it? How can I even call Harvey Harvey? Who the hell is Harvey anyway? It's frightening, isn't it, Barry, how people can be so different to how they seem.'

Tourville chose to be offended by this comment and began to flush a little. He unbuttoned his clerical collar and removed the white band he had cut from a washing-up bottle. He laid it next to the *Evening Post*, sprawled across the oak dining room table. There on the front page was a picture of Bishop Harvey looking hunted, keeping company with a tramp. Tourville began reading the headline story for the third time.

The mystery of runaway Bishop John Harvey of Southwick continues. He was spotted yesterday at Templeford Station. As first reported in the *Evening Post*, Bishop Harvey, recently consecrated at Southwick Cathedral, has left his sheep without a shepherd. A ring of silence has been carefully placed around the whole affair by Archbishop Kilgarriff and his secretary, Reverend Barry Tourville. Neither wished to comment about our most recent sighting. Unconfirmed rumours suggest that the bishop may well have been having an affair. The Archbishop has already tried to throw cold water on such rumours.

Kilgarriff turned his eyes from the garden. His flattish nose twitched as he stared hard at his secretary.

'So the fool hasn't run very far, if we are to believe the papers.'

'No,' said Tourville, scratching his high, pale brow, a prickly sweat cursing his scalp. 'I wonder if he really wanted to run away in the first place. If he did, he's making a poor job of it.' He wiped his head but the sweat quickly balled again. He was always sweating, especially when he stood next to people in crowds. Then the sweat poured off him into little rivers. The idea, never mind the feel of other people's skin, had always revolted him. Even handshaking caused him to hold his breath, decline his grey-flecked eyes, hope for a quick social execution.

Kilgarriff was different. He was physical to extremes,

especially first thing in the morning; before Mass, before six o'clock breakfast, he was out in his tracksuit, pounding down Burnt Green's sodium-lit streets. Come rain, come shine, he would be out jogging. 'Keeps the juices flowing,' he'd say to Tourville most mornings. 'You should try it, Barry, you really should. Keeps you well oiled.' But Tourville never rose to the challenge.

Now Kilgarriff took to his seat beneath his grandfather's lamp stand, brought back from Singapore years before, in sections, like a weapon. The broken vessels on his cheek and loose eyelids looked the part. Down to the knife-sharp creases in his trousers, the stubby fingers, dyed black hair, gravel voice, he was all bishop and archly so.

'I want the best the cellar's got for Monday's meeting,' he told Tourville, pausing and glaring at him. Tourville was not really listening. The sweat had only just begun to subside from his panicked skull. Now he was busy picking his nails and watching the last of the rain swish against the windows.

'Sorry, I missed that. Were you talking to me?'

'And who else? Monday's meeting,' he repeated, wondering why he had appointed such a damn fool.

'Ah, Monday, yes.'

'If you could bring up the good stuff and give Rose the day off. I don't want her to suffer the pettiness of the mob. You know what I mean. They'll be all on edge as it is. What with McNutt hovering.'

'And the food?'

Kilgarriff took his extra-long cigarettes from the chair arm, lit up, and blew an exasperated cloud up into Tourville's face.

'You know what to do, Barry. Just make sure that you get some different caterers in this time. I didn't like the last lot.'

Tourville returned to picking black oil from his fingernails. He had spent most of the day servicing Kilgarriff's blue Cambridge. It was the car he used when visiting the parishes.

It fitted the image he wanted to present: poor, humble, non-materialistic. He was none of these, of course, but the finger-marks all over the bonnet, the rust about the headlights, the dent in the boot, all convinced Southwick's parishioners that he was with them, down in the mud.

At that moment Rose came in, having knocked the door twice as was the custom. She knew that she could proceed if no objection was voiced between the first and the second knock. She brought in a tray of weak coffee which she put on the hot plate on the servery. She said nothing as she arranged the cups. Silence wrapped itself like an aura around her bony, undernourished frame. Turning on a penny, she looked briefly across at His Grace, expecting the predictable token of recognition. But this time it didn't come. Rose hung there for a moment longer than usual, but still Kilgarriff failed to flick his eyes at her. A little twitch of rejection took her face. It is enough, she told herself, to be in his shadow − in the shadow of a holy man.

Kilgarriff studied Rose from under the shelf of his thick brow. He watched the way she placed one foot before the other as a ghostly remnant of her ballet days. Then she disappeared, as all good Catholic women do.

'So, what do you think His Eminence will have to say about our runaway bishop?' asked Tourville, crossing over to the servery.

The hall clock chimed. Kilgarriff frowned, drew deeply on his low-tar, and wiped fallen ash from his chest. The pectoral cross swung to one side.

'Oh, he'll be worried about him,' he grunted. 'McNutt is very fond of Harvey. He always has been. You know how he talks. Calls him a gorgeous fellow. But a gorgeous fellow doesn't drag J C Himself through the dust. Him and his weather-house tricks. If he had stayed . . .'

'Things could have been sorted?'

'I could have moved him to another parish, kept things nice and tidy. But now the press are stiffing at his heels. And we don't want that sort of stuff out, do we? The bloody fool!'

'Sugar?'

'Of course I want sugar. I always have sugar. When have you seen me not taking sugar?'

Tourville allowed himself a camp shrug at this outburst. It was the kind of camp gesture that marked seminary life; rarely homosexual, just playing at it. He was never brave enough to take a position. He stirred the coffee and took it over to Kilgarriff, who was just finishing a string of curses against Harvey. But Tourville thought his mumbling was against him. He handed the cup over rather abruptly and left the room with a lemon in his mouth.

Kilgarriff didn't even notice that his secretary was upset. He slurped the coffee through his tense lips, staring out over the rim at the rain-laced lawn, thinking of Harvey.

'The guy's an arsehole,' he hissed.

After coffee, Kilgarriff retired upstairs to his study. He was reluctant to do any work, but he had been writing a rejoinder to an article about poor church attendance figures. He sat down at his desk, switched on the lamp and scanned the latest figures of *Pastoral Statistics*. They were boring and depressing. With storm clouds outside his window, it was times like this when Kilgarriff wanted to hang up his collar. The figures were awful. Attendance had dropped across the Archdiocese of Southwick by fifteen per cent. Fifteen per cent in one year! Only one-twelfth of the Catholic population came to Mass each week. Kilgarriff pulled at his mastiff jaw and envisioned all his stock of buildings standing idle like empty warehouses.

Throughout Southwick, he had to juggle those clergy not yet laicised or retired due to old age or sickness, sending them from parish to parish, trying to keep roofs from caving in, wood from rotting, floors from sinking. The Catholic schools struggled. In England, the Church was finally looking weak, a pale shadow of its glory days. Bedraggled, unsure of itself, it sang the same old tunes with devastating effect. And so, in the years since *Vatican II*, half the priests of Southwick had left the ministry. In the world, one hundred and fifty thousand priests had left the altar in the time it took a baby to be called a man.

But what could he do? Nothing, except fight on in defence of the Faith. And this he did ruthlessly. He kept his priests in fear of a telephone call. He intimidated them. He assigned them to backwaters if any opened their mouths too widely. For the Church was collapsing. There was no doubt about that. It wore the dodo smile. And he, like many others, did not want to find out why. He put on the blinkers he had been trained to run with.

Now Kilgarriff felt particularly keen to wield his shrinking yet still considerable power. He thumbed through his thick telephone book and called one of his two hundred priests. The statistics had provoked him into action. The phone rang in a presbytery at the furthest reach of the Archdiocese. He waited. The housekeeper answered it.

'I want to speak to Father David,' he told her.

'Oh yes, now if you would just wait a moment I'll go and see if I can find him for you. Hold on.' The housekeeper was not the least bit aware of who was on the phone.

While Kilgarriff listened to nothing he looked out over Burnt Green in all its suburban banality and wished for persecutions again, real bloody ones. He would have liked to have had to hide in holes, tell secret Masses, and all that. Outside, the sodium lamps fizzed tartrazine into the blue night. In Kilgarriff's half closed eyes, they became flaming torches of a Protestant mob, coming to flush him out. The dream was all he had. There were no signs of the old, hard won Faith in the rain-skinned streets below. There was no spark of commitment.

'Hello,' said Father David at St Martha's.

Kilgarriff pressed the receiver into his ear.

'Hello, David, how are you?'

David recognised the voice. 'I'm fine, Your Grace. How are you?'

Kilgarriff didn't answer on purpose. He liked to pickle his priests in silence. Father David interrupted the silence with a cough or two.

'Now, David, I want you to move up to St Bernard's.'

Father David's voice lost weight.

'St Bernard's? Move? But I've only been at St Martha's nine months. Now that I'm settled into the parish, I think . . .'

'Well, now look, David, I'm afraid we have to go where we are sent. There's no time for settling.'

'But – '

'By next Sunday, David, okay? I must get off now. I'll speak with you again.'

Kilgarriff replaced the receiver and then began to take another look at the *Pastoral Statistics* and *Annuarium Statisticum Ecclesiae*. What did numbers matter anyway, he told himself. If there were only a handful of Catholics left in England, so be it. He was sick and tired of massaging the figures. But he would do it if needed. Deny a problem exists. That is the quickest solution. They had done the same for years with the paedophile priests.

Downstairs, Tourville licked bits of sugar from his coffee cup and felt the deep aching in his groin. He ignored it as long as he could, but knew that he would submit to its call. It was inevitable. He could not wrong-foot it. He would think about something else, anything, but the thoughts would boomerang and the ache would grow again like a pleasurable cancer. Now

31

his throat began to bump with his heart. He felt queasy and parted his thin, unloved lips, always a white fur of spit at the corners. He took the last of the sugar, trying to distract himself by looking out at the whipping rain. There was no hope of resisting the ache. He was losing control. He had needs like any other man, he told himself as the cup rattled in its saucer.

He stood up and moved quickly out of the room and along the hall, leaping up the luxuriously carpeted stairwell, two steps at a time. He clasped his hands in front of him and bit his lip. He just hoped to God that Kilgarriff didn't interrupt him now. Not now that he had given the ache a free rein. It seemed an age before he reached the sanctuary of his barn-like room, where he rushed and knelt down beside his bed.

He held his hands so tightly that his fingernails blanched. He knew he would give in, but he wanted one last gesture of self-control. 'Control the body,' his mother whispered deep inside his head. 'Control the body.' But his fingers were already holding the little metal tag of his fly zip. I have the same needs, he told himself, tugging downwards. His other hand was busily searching from side to side under the mattress. Now his cock was pointing upwards. It was thin and bent like a stick in water. It was crying a single tear.

Tourville heard the knock at his door. He panicked, but the panic was too long and unproductive. His hand was still under the heavy mattress. His cock was still up like the finger of a holy man. Rose was at the door. It was her knock. And she would enter with the second tap. Tourville's tongue began to shout out. But it was too late. Tourville would have to improvise.

When Rose entered with her second knock, Tourville had managed to retrieve his hand from under the mattress and bring his joined hands above his head as if he were performing the most exhausting of prayers.

'Sorry, Father,' Rose whispered when she saw him on his

knees. She stood with her back foot out sideways and front foot pointing, as if she might carry out her ballet routine at any moment. 'I didn't know you were – I know what it's like when you're lost in prayer.'

'What do you want?' hissed Tourville.

'There are some ladies at the door, father. I thought you had better deal with them. His Grace is not to be disturbed. They are – well, you can just hear them.'

Tourville was at a critical point. The sound of Rose's voice hadn't helped. Now other women's voices added to his ache. He shuddered suddenly, involuntarily and suppressed a moan.

'Yes, all right. I'll be along in a moment,' he croaked.

Rose smiled admiringly and left the room sideways.

When finally Tourville went downstairs, disgusted with himself for having given in to the ache, he was met with the faces of real, not imagined women. He felt transparent. Could they read from his face what he had been doing just moments before? Had he left a residue? Quickly he looked down and wiped at his black trousers.

The women were out on the gravel, shuffling in the cold, and singing a chant in a ragged way. Something about 'opportunity'. For a few moments he thought 'carol singers', but this was highly unlikely. Not that it was too early for them, but that they should come all the way up the hill from the village to sing to the Archbishop. He had never witnessed such an event in his fourteen years as secretary. That never happened. It would be like preaching to God. And Kilgarriff was God in his way, on his hill, always descending. Even his handshake had to come down a long way, like a plane landing, never across like a brother, or from below like a servant.

Barely recovering his usual equanimity, Tourville smiled falsely and patronised them.

'Good evening, ladies, and how are we?'

He could almost feel the breath of the largest member of the group as she barked up at him.

'We've brought a petition,' she said, her chin lifting to meet his, a glitter in her eyes which Tourville mistook for feminine submissiveness.

'Ah,' he said. 'How nice of you all to come along. Where are you from? Which parish? What are we about? Is it the Grants for Catholic Schools Campaign? But you said you have a petition. How interesting.' He was stooping as low as possible, looking about him from under his strong brow, melting his spine for effect.

The forthright woman who had spoken dropped a pile of signed papers at his feet. Two more were thrown forward from the little crowd.

'Let's see,' said Tourville. 'Now, what is this all about?'

The women began crunching the gravel to keep warm. Tourville regained his spine when he saw the words 'Women for the Priesthood' on the papers.

'There are,' began the spokeswoman, 'six thousand eight hundred and five signatures approving the ordination of women. You can't say the Church doesn't need us.'

'I can and I do,' answered Tourville immediately. 'And I'm sure His Grace will say exactly the same.' The spokeswoman moved from under Tourville's shower of spittle. A little of the spume he generated floated down onto her scalp-tight black hair.

Then she turned and with the others just stormed off, leaving Tourville with a flea in his ear, standing dismayed on the doorstep. He watched as the intruder light in the driveway came on and lit up bobble hats, coats, skirts and boots slipping away behind the trees. They neither spoke nor looked back. In silence, they trudged the gravel.

Tourville shook his head and cursed under his breath, vague memories of the spokeswoman returning. Years ago, she had lectured at a conference about the ordination of women. As he bent down to pick up the bundles of petitions, he chased images of her in his mind. He saw her now on the podium: her eyes blue-soft, her flowing black hair, her light harmless voice. Of course, she was put in her place as he remembered. Put down well and truly. And by other women, which was even better. What did she expect? Then there was that buffet afterwards to help remove the heart for change once the steam had been let out of the protest group. Plenty of wine had been served up to induce sleep and forgetfulness.

With that thought, Tourville walked round to the side of the house and dumped the petitions in the dustbin. Hunching his shoulders, he pushed them as far down as they would go. It was ridiculous to talk of women priests. And as for married priests – the Church would simply not be able to afford it.

At that moment the gravel crunched with the approach of a car. Tourville quickly put the lid on the bin and moved into the headlights of a Morris Minor. It was Rose's daughter. He sneered when he saw her but quickly broadened a smile. He waited as Mildred slowly wound down the window, struggling with a stiff handle. She turned down the dance music and slipped another CD disk into the player that rested on the back seat.

'Hi,' she said, 'I suppose Mum is finishing off the dishes from supper.'

Tourville held his distance. Mildred had a friend with her, someone that Tourville had never seen before. Tourville squinted through the windscreen and made out the young black face, luminescent yellow jacket, and a spike of bangled hair. She looked like a traffic cone, Tourville thought.

'I'm sure she'll be out in a little while,' he said, beginning to move away. As he turned his back, Mildred and her friend burst out laughing.

'I told you, Flipper, he's a real fart.'

Flipper sucked her teeth and shook her head. She turned up the music. That brought Tourville back to the car. He stuck his head just close enough to Mildred for his bad breath to carry.

'It's a bit loud,' he said.

Flipper reached back and turned it right down.

'That's better, thank you.'

Tourville left them again, Mildred wafting the air in front of her face. Flipper turned up the music and then got into the back to leave the front seat free for Rose. Tourville stopped for a moment but then carried on into the house.

'Can you imagine taking that to bed?' said Mildred.

'Nah,' answered Flipper, cranking up the bass.

'I bet it's all, you know, shrivelled.'

They both laughed at the thought.

'I couldn't stand that breath,' Flipper shouted above the music.

'God, it was awful, wasn't it? It really stank.'

Flipper turned the music up even louder, threatening to shake some of the rust from the Morris Minor.

'They're all the same, man, those vicars,' said Flipper.

'Some are nice.'

'And how would you know?'

Mildred laughed and, reaching round, thumped Flipper on the arm. Mildred's fist sank into the luminescent quilting. Flipper gave her a backhand across the top of her head.

'Well, you go on about them an awful lot. I thought you might have some real experience, you know what I mean?'

'Here's Mum.'

Rose was standing in the hallway. Tourville was talking to her. She hardly bruised the carpet, she was so frail. Tourville raised his hand. She nodded and he closed the door after her.

★

36

At five o'clock the following morning, Kilgarriff was in his light blue tracksuit and training shoes. He jogged across the driveway, the intruder light picking him out, making him conspicuous to no one under the dark sky. Few people were up at this hour. It was the monk in Kilgarriff that made him favour a dawn start. He lifted his knees more than usual, puffing from his mouth rhythmically, bounding forth onto the hill. Today he chose Route One, the most difficult of his circuits. He wanted the hardest workout this morning. He wanted to bleed his system, force it to respond, even if it killed him. For later that day he had to visit the parish at Hickley and tidy up after Harvey. The parishioners needed reassurance. The sheep needed to be calmed. He would soften them up, set them on their knees, get them to think about their own sins and fail to see those of Bishop Harvey. Get them looking at their boots and shoes, instead of up, up, up. He would lie to them as best he could. He would give them as many lies as God could bestow upon him.

Kilgarriff always paid particular attention to his breathing during his jogging. He liked his breaths to come in a clock-work, measured way as he paced the hill, keeping to the edge of forest. It was a long climb but satisfying. He liked pain. Pain was a reminder of being alive.

After some time, he was puffing for air. The military precision of his lungs gave way. His flesh dropped and swung to the side as his feet pounded into the tarmac. His loose cheeks jigged blood to the surface. Still, the hill wound ever upwards, it seemed, forcing Kilgarriff to dip his head and eventually swing it from side to side, as if he were boxing frantically. He summoned his muscles to flex and stretch. But the fat on his heavily-built frame would not make light work of it. Refusing to stop and draw proper breaths, he spun round and jogged backwards, bringing his knees up as far as possible, defying a heart attack. He looked down over the rooftops of

Burnt Green, chastising his failing body to fight on, to go on in style. 'One, two, one, two,' he chanted, his lungs like damp, hot flannels behind his ribs. He brought in the Trinity: 'One, two, three, one, two, three.' It seemed to help. And then he broke into his favourite verse:

> *Jog on, jog on, the footpath way*
> *And merrily hent the stile-a.*
> *A merry heart goes all the day,*
> *Your sad tires in a mile-a.*

On he went, his knees creaking, nose dribbling, till he reached the top of the hill. Normally, he would have stopped for breath at this point and denied later that he ever had, for his body's collapse was to be lied about, covered up. 'Fit as a fiddle,' he announced to no one, jogging on the spot, looking out over the vacant picnic spot, out over the dark fields below. He wondered in which direction Templeford lay, and scratched compass points onto the underside of his skull. West, he decided. His eyes looked west, skirting Burnt Green Station, over the barely visible fields, beyond Hickley Beacon. All hidden behind that high shelf of land came Hickley, Stonehill, and finally Templeford. Kilgarriff could hear the milk float clinking in the streets below. He stopped for a moment and looked at his watch, squeezing a button to light up the face. He was slow today.

The remainder of Route One was easy, all downhill, north-wards for a while and then bending eastwards along a dirt track that spiralled down to the one side of Archbishop's House. Kilgarriff managed a little sprint during the descent, then tempered the pace as the jolting threatened to bring on his back trouble. Leaping from side to side to avoid the muddy runnel along the middle of the track, he almost ended up in the hedges and barbed wire. When finally he reached the house he slowed to walking pace, easing his breath, wiping the sweat from his face, preparing to show Rose and Tourville a calmed entrance, a picture of health. But he never accounted for his beetroot complexion. It would be an hour or more before the blood left the surface of his face.

4

Harvey woke to the sound of sizzling oil. He sat up perplexed, not simply by the smell, but by the obvious absence of Crystal. Throwing clear the few blankets that had barely kept him warm during the night, Harvey rose to his feet, settled his balance, and crossed the floor. He stumbled towards the cubbyhole and found the cooker raging beneath a blackened, smoking pan. He cut the gas and wondered why Crystal had left it on. But the thought was replaced by the idea of a cooked breakfast. Harvey felt very hungry. The smoking oil brought images of fried bacon, sausages and egg. Just an egg, he thought, would be marvellous. With the cold at his back and with apparitions of food in the cooling pan, he began his day with a sense of harshness and abandonment. All the years of cooked breakfasts and the comfortable priestly life haunted him.

He turned away swiftly and started to clap heat into his frozen fingers. He wished the despair he felt was quite so easy to dispel. He went to the dusty window and looked out. He looked anywhere, it didn't matter. As long as he looked he could give his mind its work to do. What the hell was he doing here, he pondered. In a mental hostel, or whatever it was called, miles from anyone he knew. After a restless night, his eyes felt sore, like grit-coated pebbles. He blinked them and swallowed dryly. How on earth had he come to this?

Below, East Vale spread its brick before him. The late,

winter dawn had hardly broken. A yellow light came from the open door of a paper shop further down the street, its jaundice cutting across the deserted pavement.

Harvey looked beyond the street to the three high-rise blocks, falling in a line towards Templeford, and north-east to the shimmering reservoir and gasworks, then finally north-west to two church spires huddled together by perspective only. When Harvey saw these he averted his eyes.

Back down the street, Harvey caught sight of Crystal emerging suddenly from the entry to a gully. Yes, it was definitely him. His oilskins gleamed briefly in the light from the paper shop. His gumboots chafed the puddles that littered his path back to the hostel. He was carrying a bag. Harvey quickly moved from the window and sat on the edge of the sofa. All of a sudden he was afraid at the arrival of his strange host. Perhaps it was time to leave, he thought. Why delay? The guy was mad. Who knows, perhaps he had killed someone?

At the thought, Harvey instinctively reached for his coat and began to scout for his umbrella and holdall. He fumbled and panicked. Perhaps Crystal was bringing back a child's head in that bag. Get out! he urged himself. Out! Out! Now! But time had squeezed a tightrope for him to escape upon. It was as if he were meant to stay. Already, Crystal was letting himself in through the main door. Now his boots were on the stairs. Harvey dropped his coat and holdall onto the sofa and submitted, striking an innocent pose beside the empty grate. The sound of Crystal clearing his throat curled into Harvey's ears, and then the door opened. 'Fate,' he whispered to himself.

When the door opened, Harvey's upturned eyes tried to look at ease with the world, as if he had just been considering how to light a fire to warm the room.

'What's that smoke?' asked Crystal immediately.

'You left the pan on.'

41

Crystal shrugged, sniffed the air again and placed the bag he was carrying on the sideboard.

'Oh, I forgot,' he said, beginning to laugh in a strangely false kind of way. 'You see, I began to make breakfast, and realized there was nothing in the fridge to eat.'

Fridge? Harvey could see no fridge. Perhaps it was downstairs – a communal fridge to go with the communal toilet and bathroom.

Crystal slipped out of his oilskin jacket, tightened the string around his leggings and opened the bag. Harvey squirmed a little from the projection of his imagination, but there was no child's head. Just some very streaky bacon, some ragged sausages, half a loaf of bread and a carton of milk.

'I hope you don't mind,' he said, holding out a fist of change, 'but I took ten pounds out of your coat pocket.'

Harvey just stared at him.

'I thought you wouldn't mind. After all, you looked kind of hungry. And I was afraid to wake you and ask.'

Harvey's mouth opened but nothing came out. At first, as always, he burned inside. Eventually he picked up his coat and searched the pockets.

'That's all I took,' said Crystal, taking the bacon and sausages through into the cubbyhole.

Harvey had a vain hope that there might be some other money crumpled into the corners of his pockets. A tightly folded note, perhaps. Or one worn to softness. But there was nothing. Crystal had taken and spent most of his last tenner.

'You went through my pockets, just like that,' chided Harvey. 'You went through my private things? How dare you? You had no right!'

Crystal popped his head from out of the cubbyhole. He was shocked to hear the bishop venting his anger.

'You took my last ten pounds. That's all I had.'

Crystal squinted, grimaced.

'That was all I had between myself and the gutter.'

'Ah,' said Crystal. 'Ah.'

'Ah,' repeated Harvey louder with venom.

'I thought, er, you had plenty. You know, with that watch and ring and everything.'

Harvey was shaking his head at him.

'You looked hungry,' Crystal told him. He held the frying pan out towards him. 'Smell that,' he said.

Harvey sat on the arm of the sofa and stared at the grimy stripes on the carpet where the floorboards showed through like a brass rubbing. His head fell into his hands, yet he knew that Crystal had meant well. He hadn't stolen the money as such. Besides, a tenner was next to nothing anyway. It was hardly a safety net. And he had spent the money on food. Eventually, he lifted a hand of apology.

'I'm touchy,' he said. 'Sorry. The food smells great.'

Crystal smiled his unsmile and returned to the cooking.

'What the hell's happening to me?' Harvey mumbled to himself. 'My whole world's collapsing around me.' But he didn't want to go over everything again. He pushed the grey hair back over his scalp, and began to wash his face with air.

Crystal took a fresh box of matches, courtesy of Harvey, and lit some newspaper in the grate, setting unburned remains of wood on top, before finally adding some sugar which flared up and created much, but momentary, heat. Then, without further ado, he went into the cubbyhole, reheated the pan, and cooked some of the bacon and sausage. The remainder he put in a carrier bag and hung outside the sash window, where the cold air provided a poor man's fridge.

With a lump of bread, a cut of bacon and several sausages on his plate, Harvey felt better. His fears about Crystal's violent side seemed overplayed. His image of him softened. Crystal had not only given Harvey a bed for the night but had cooked him breakfast. Of course, Harvey would not have gone out of his way to keep such company, but even so, now that he had it, he was grateful. After all, he could have spent the night in a shop alcove or the station waiting room.

Thinking things over as he wolfed down his sausages and dipped his bread in the grease, Harvey began to look less unfavourably on his host. The steaming cup of tea that Crystal soon thrust into his hand helped this feeling even more. The upper room of the hostel became more friendly, less alien. There was little difference between this meal and those he had been served in various refectories. More dirt and grime, of course. No silver napkin rings. No letters. No newspapers. But the essentials were there. Hot greasy food and tea.

He gladly ate what Crystal offered him. Crystal went up in his estimation. Yes, he was mad. But who wasn't these days? Yet he had fed him. He was the first person in days to show any concern. In Stonehill, in Metchley, no one had batted an eyelid. He could go shit himself and die, and no one would have cared. The thought made him shiver. He feared a lonely death more than anything. With this thought he nearly choked on a lump of bread.

'Are you always strapped for cash?' he asked Crystal.

'Always.'

'So how do you manage?'

'This and that, you know. I get benefits. Only the landlady has most of that. The rest, well, I like to smoke.'

'What about food?'

'I manage,' Crystal told him. 'I beg. The old soup stuff and that. I manage, don't worry about me. No one else does.'

'I know that feeling,' said Harvey.

'But you're a bishop.'

'Was, Crystal, was.' He looked through the gridiron of carpet, imagining the landlady down there counting her money.

'You like my cooking?'

'Yes, Crystal, I like your cooking. Thank you.'

'I'm sure you're used to better,' sniffed Crystal.

'Well, yes, but this is just fine, really.'

'I suppose,' said Crystal, a hint of regret in his voice, for he was one of the loneliest of men, 'you'll be on your way, wherever that is.'

Harvey picked up the undertow of his words and chewed it out with a piece of bacon rind. He could barely feel the weight of the loose change hanging in his pocket. It wouldn't get him far. Certainly, he would have to sell his ring, the watch or pectoral cross before doing anything. For a moment he even considered how much the gold filigree on his mitre could be worth. Not a lot, surely.

Swallowing the fat, he looked at Crystal, who stared away through the window. Crystal's blistered lip hung loose, and filthy hair caught the steam from his mug of tea. Harvey felt sorry for him, despite himself. He had spent most of his life talking about the poor and precious little time reaching out to them. The religious motive had always ruined his occasional generosity – a spike in his giving hand.

'Well?' said Crystal, turning his face from the window, his eyes dim and sunken. 'Which way are you heading?'

Harvey thought again about Montgomery. He questioned the asylum he would find in his company. Would Montgomery bail him out? Would he be at his last address? Would there be a bed for him there? Harvey reached into his pocket and drew out the little discoloured white taxi-card. Montgomery's address had been scribbled out on the back. There was no phone number. He had taken his details in a chance meeting six years ago. He could be anywhere now.

'I'll have to get some money first,' Harvey said at last, taking a quick swig of his tea. 'I can't go anywhere until I do that.'

Crystal thought Harvey was having another go at him for taking his last tenner and spending most of it.

'I wish I hadn't bothered making you breakfast,' he said.

'No, I'm not getting at you,' Harvey told him. 'That tenner wasn't going to help, was it? I need *real* money. I'll have to sell something.'

'To buy clothes?'

'Clothes?'

'You kept talking in your sleep about buying new clothes. Nothing purple, nothing black, you kept saying over and over again. Normal clothes. Something less conspicuous.'

Harvey blushed. He had forgotten how he talked in his sleep.

'Did I say anything else?'

'You just mumbled a lot. About, well, I don't know what. You said a whole heap of rubbish.'

Harvey laughed thinly and pulled at his black shirt and trousers.

'Normal clothes, eh?'

'Yeah, that's what you said.'

Crystal polished off a sausage, jamming it sideways into his mouth. He talked with his mouth full.

'How will you get money?'

Harvey shrugged but looked instantly at his ring.

'I guess I could sell this,' he told him.

'Nice.'

'Or this?' Harvey drew up his sleeve and revealed the gold watch.

'Very nice.'

Harvey didn't show Crystal the huge, thick-chained pectoral cross that he wore under his shirt. It was an outrageous piece of jewellery. It must have cost a fortune. But he did not feel he could sell that. The idea seemed blasphemous somehow.

Crystal still talked as he chewed his food.

'You should get good money for those, I'm telling you.'

'Well, as long as I have enough to get me to London and keep me fed and dry for a while.'

'And the clothes. Don't forget the new clothes.'

'No, and new clothes.'

Crystal swallowed.

'So you'll be off soon, then?'

'Yep.'

For a while both men kept silent. Harvey polished the last of the grease from his plate. Crystal magicked a bent nub from somewhere and lit up. His words came on a cloud of stale smoke.

'I'll take you down to the jewellery quarter, then,' he said trying to straighten the nub, heedless of the hot tip. 'Not really a quarter. A few shops, that's all. But that's what they call it round here. You should get a reasonable price for the ring or watch. Then, what day is it? Wednesday. The market will be open. You'll be able to get some cheap clothes there. Second-hand stuff even, at the charity shops. There are lots of them in Templeford.'

'I noticed,' said Harvey. 'And shoe shops.'

Crystal couldn't help feeling sorry for Harvey falling on hard times and being a bishop and all. He had certainly fallen a long way. Crystal blew smoke down his nostrils and shook his head, looking across at the forlorn figure with grey hair and spiking chin. A bishop, who would have thought it? A bishop, here, at the hostel. Christ, it was laughable. There on his white marble hand, a ring of office. Crystal had kissed one of those years ago in another life. That was long before he was committed to Roney Hill Asylum and paraldehyde injections took Jesus away.

'And you,' Harvey asked. 'What about you? You could do with some – '

But Harvey thought better of saying what he thought.

'What?'

'Nothing.'

'What? What could I do with?'

Harvey coughed.

'I'm sure the oilskins are practical and everything, but all the same.'

'Can't beat them,' said Crystal. 'But if you're buying. Well, I could do with a few undergarments. A hat, even, before the winter really sets in good and proper. But I won't hold my breath. You might get less money than you imagine. They're tight-fisted buggers down the quarter, I can tell you that for nothing.'

'Well, we'll see. Anyway, I'm sure whatever I get will stretch to a hat. They must have some at the charity shops.'

Harvey put his plate down on the floor. For a moment he imagined Crystal wearing his mitre. And why not? he asked himself. Could a more worthy bishop be found? Would Southwick suffer more under him than it did under me? With this thought he twisted his ring of office till the garnet looked inwards, out of view. He would have removed it there and then, but for the fatness of his finger. It would need soap or spittle, he decided.

Despite Harvey's wish to discuss the previous day's events with Crystal, he found that he could not broach the subject, even during the long walk that afternoon to Templeford market. Thus, for the time being, it remained a mystery as to why Crystal had stopped him catching his train, why he had acted so bizarrely, why he talked of frustrated time, lost forever, never to be replaced. Why, in short, he had wasted his time. Obviously, it was something to do with his madness.

They passed through East Vale, keeping their faces downcast as wind cut from the north and whirled eastwards. It felt like it might begin to snow. Crystal drew in his collar, his fag burning all the faster in the blow of wind, whistling at his ears, bullying a tear from his eye which tracked upwards onto his scalp. He nearly lost his roach several times, having to bite to keep it. Past the Three Ships they went. These high-rise flats with stinking lifts and porthole windows needed knocking down. Now and then, Harvey caught a face looking out briefly. Looking out at what? Certainly not the sea. This was landlocked England. Perhaps they were looking out for the orange trams that Templeford Council had brought back from the claws of history. But apart from these streetcars, little else of interest happened in Templeford to excite the eye.

The road into town was long and dipping, flattening out quickly as it hit the Six Ways roundabout. The hill made the eastbound trams struggle while the westbound trams flew. In fact, East Vale deserved no such name, for it lay on higher ground than Templeford. The terminus for East Vale trams stood where the road levelled out. It was here that Harvey followed Crystal across the lines and past Woolworths. As he caught up with him and they walked along the street together, Harvey felt it had been such a long time since he had stopped at the B&B. But it was only yesterday.

Wondering what the pair of them looked like – one all in black with grey hair, the other in oilskins – he was glad to walk quickly through the crowds. As he did so, he felt like a rag of shadow that Crystal was trying desperately to shake off. The pace took his breath but he didn't lag behind. He just wanted to get through to the market, where they might blend in with the least prosperous inhabitants.

Harvey kept alongside Crystal as they went past the last row of buildings, mostly charity and shoe shops. Uncomfortable at feeling so conspicuous, he dropped back a little from Crystal as if to say that he was his own man and not at all connected with the tramp ahead of him. But still people stared. And how they stared! Harvey took it badly, but not Crystal. Crystal was used to it by now. He let the stares just roll off his oilskin. He accepted himself as outcast. There were more disturbing things in his life than disapproving stares. Much more disturbing things. He knew that only too well.

Crystal didn't notice Harvey's unease. He did not much care that Harvey held back from him. Everyone else did. Why should Harvey be any different? When Harvey looked up, the people seemed to rush away, or move backwards, almost evaporate. Of course, they didn't move as dramatically as this, but that is how Harvey felt. It was his nerves, and he had plenty of them at the moment. The people he saw all appeared light, ghostlike, the wind rolling them out of view.

No sooner had they reached the B&B Harvey had stayed in the night before than Crystal was distracted. On the far side of the bridge he saw a woman coming to blows with her enormous suitcase that lay on its side on the flagstones. She was kicking it in the ribs as if it were an exhausted little donkey. At first Crystal was a bit shocked by the venom the woman showed in her attack. He blinked several times, just watching as she dug at the suitcase again with her foot. When the beast did not rise she started tugging it towards the railway station. Now and again she shook her stinging fingers. Down in the station her train appeared to strain like an athlete at the blocks. It looked about to move off. It looked ready, and she was not down there. She lifted the suitcase in mad little desperate hops, cursing as she went. It was then that Crystal moved in, quite forgetting that Harvey was in tow. He just had to do what he had to do.

He knew only too well by her panicky glances down into the station and up at the station clock that she was cutting it fine. Crystal licked the blister on his lip and smiled. How easy his work came to him in this modern day rush, rush, rush. The sand in the hourglass. Her blood hissing down through that narrow neck. Time had found an excruciating pressure point. That was time's gift. Time evaporating and opportunity with it. He could see that the woman was growing more and more

When he did finally speak, he told Harvey that he just had to do certain things and couldn't go into details. He kept looking up to the right, and Harvey couldn't help suspecting that Crystal was hearing voices.

A tram pulled out from the westbound terminus, heading past St Agatha's and the old market. Metchley via Stonehill, the board on the front read. Its bell sounded as it merged with the traffic. Again, Harvey was dismayed at ending up in Templeford. He felt lost. Hickley seemed far off, and Southwick Cathedral with its high white tower and buttresses was another world away. His fingers had lost the cool touch of the chalice and the leathery comfort of the breviary. He kept company with a schizophrenic, surely, and a chronic one at that. And a time-waster.

'It's just something I have to do,' Crystal told him after an extended silence. He slouched away guiltily, dragging his gumboots across the flagstones.

'Really?' jabbed Harvey. 'This is how you spend your day? Stopping people going about their business? That woman?' Harvey felt a pang of fear all of a sudden. He sensed that he might inflame the unpredictable Crystal. He knew of several cases of violent attacks on innocent members of the public by ex-mental patients living in the community. And after all, Harvey barely knew him. But Crystal did not react. In fact, he seemed quite agreeable, turning to Harvey and shrugging his shoulders.

'As I said, it's something I have to do,' he told him. 'I don't mean to harm anyone.' At this point Crystal looked up and away from Harvey and mumbled. 'No more. Not today.' Then he turned his face on Harvey. 'Come on,' he said. 'I'll take you to the jewellery quarter.'

He moved between the black taxis lined up in the plaza and headed down towards the old market. The taxis reminded Harvey of the little card Montgomery had given him with his

helpless. The frustrated grimace on her face showed that she had begun to accept that she would miss her train. That was no good to Crystal. He must change that attitude. He must give her a little bit of hope.

Crystal approached her, standing as she did at the gutter's edge, complaining to herself about her sore fingers which had moulded into the shape of the hard suitcase handle and become temporarily contracted. She smoothed them with her other hand. She knew she should have asked the taxi driver to help, or allowed more time, or asked a station porter, if they still existed, to bring a barrow of some kind. But it was too late now. She could imagine her plane at Heathrow filling with everyone except her. Her sunshine winter break was slipping away. As far as Crystal was concerned, he could sense that she was just dangling, just ripe for the picking.

'Can I help?' he offered.

At first a flash of disgust crossed the woman's face, but then she weighed everything up. This rag of humanity would do the job.

'Oh, my God, yes, thank you, please,' she said pulling back her sweaty hair and dancing around the massive case. 'I'm going to miss my train. I just can't lift this anymore. It's so heavy, damn it!'

'Well now, let me see,' said Crystal, taking his time to wrap his fist around the handle. Even this small delay brought a slash of pain to the woman's face.

'I'm late,' she said. 'Terribly late, please.'

Crystal gave a glimmer of a smile, an almost extinct smile.

'I thought so,' he said. 'I couldn't help but notice. Now, is there anything, you know, fragile inside?'

'No, no, just hurry up,' said the woman. 'Please, I've got a plane to catch.'

'Now don't worry, there's plenty of time,' he told her. 'When did you say your train is going?'

'In three minutes,' said the woman desperately.

'We should make it,' Crystal reassured her, lifting the case with his powerful arm and walking towards the entrance. The woman gasped with relief. 'It's a heavy case you've got here,' he said, swinging it. 'There isn't a body in it, is there?'

'No, no, it just feels like it. Now, please hurry,' she said as she shooed a group of people out of their way. She almost laid a hand on Crystal's back to push him along, but thought better of it. If he had looked at her he would have seen her narrowed, desperate eyes with lashes like wasp stings. But he didn't need to look. He knew the symptoms. He had given her hope *against* time. He had brought the pain of hope back into her day.

'I'll have to stop for a second,' Crystal told her. 'My lungs aren't as good as they used to be.'

The woman nearly exploded.

'My train!' she croaked. 'Don't stop, please, please.'

Crystal picked up the suitcase again, and she stopped grinding her teeth and began to whip her hand at the air in front of Crystal, egging him on. Up till now she had not cared to look at Crystal. But now she was willing the grubby man in oilskins and shorn-off gumboots to get that suitcase down the stairs. Her grimace deepened. Her teeth showed as if she had been suddenly poisoned. Crystal became a silly scarecrow struggling on purpose to get the suitcase down, down, down.

'Look, you stupid man, can't you hurry up? I'll miss my train if you don't get a move on!'

Now Crystal slowed down altogether. He felt her distress. He smelt it. He saw frustrated clots of time falling away. The sweat bled from her. The woman jumped up and down now at his sluggish progress. She sensed that down below, beneath the canopy, the train threatened to jolt away at any second.

'Move!' she scolded him.

They were on the platform now. And there was the train.

'Here we are,' he said, putting the case down. The suddenly rushed towards the train, waving madly and at the guard at the far end of the train. She returne case and Crystal.

'Damn it! Come on, please,' she growled at hin further inarticulate sounds. Her head jerked as she s Crystal's face, as if she could thrust her hand into head and take control. A prickling sensation ran acro scalp. He looked up at the station clock and felt th of time. He turned and apologised briefly that he c more to help her. And that is how he left her. In a hold of the case herself, and for an illusory mome capable of tucking it under her arm and running But the suitcase dug its heels into the platform her.

Harvey followed Crystal down onto the platfor walking away from the woman. The woman was now and looking up at the clock as she dragge inch by inch closer to the train. But even the keen to speed up and prevent her from reach Crystal had the same wounded look that Harve his face the day before, after he had stopped h train. Before Harvey could lend the woman a the guard blew his whistle and the train moved

'That was nasty,' Crystal said brushing past, with himself. 'But if I don't do it, *they* will . short his words and climbed back up the stairs station without bothering to see if Harvey wa was, still wondering what on earth he was doi low company. The truth was he was intrigue caught up with him.

'What's going on with you?' he asked hin looked back at him suspiciously, gazed up second or two, and then turned on his heel t

address on it. It was still in his pocket. And he felt more and more that staying with Montgomery would be the best start to a new life. First, however, he would go and see what he could get for his ring or watch. He was tired and lonely, despite Crystal's company. He decided he could do with some *real* company. But for now he would go with the flow, take one day at a time, let one leg follow the other and see where he ended up.

Crystal was still talking to himself, and when he stopped suddenly and looked back the way they had come, Harvey followed his gaze. He seemed to be looking out towards a high wooded hill a mile or so out of town along East Vale.

'What are you looking at?' he asked him.

'Roney Hill,' Crystal told him, dabbing his lip. 'Roney Hill Asylum. Closed now.'

'They're all closing, aren't they?' Harvey said. 'A bit like the dissolution of the monasteries.'

'The what?'

'Henry the Eighth got rid of the monasteries. Closed them down.'

Roney Hill had been closed and stood empty for years. The Prison Service almost took it over, and then a hotel chain, but in the end no one wanted it. Only the front of the building remained. It resembled Bath Crescent, though a more down-market version. Built in 1818, it was one of the earliest asylums in the country. At one time, horse-drawn carriages with new inmates would have trundled over the lock-up cells beneath the crescent driveway and brought the traditional Roney Hill welcome: screaming. Now the asylum was largely demolished except for the tiny chapel which, like the front of the asylum, had a preservation order served on it. The free land was still for sale, but no one was building these days.

'You were there?' Harvey asked him. His question seemed to lose itself in the channel of air between them.

'What?'

'Roney Hill. You were there?'

'Oh, I was there.' He waved his hand, erasing the view, and turned. 'I was on long stay. But not for long. I had just got used to the place, you know, working even. Worked down at the concrete unit, making slabs and fence posts. Then just like that we were all discharged.'

He walked fast now over the cobbles and back down towards the market square. Harvey caught up with him. Crystal seemed eager to escape, charging off into the crowds of shoppers, Harvey slipping off his oily back. Harvey could see the disdainful way people stared as Crystal passed, and then felt little changed in their faces when he followed in his wake. They think I'm mad too, Harvey suspected. Well, maybe I am. Isn't everyone?

People got out of Crystal's way as if he were torching them. Harvey had an easy passage through to the other side of the market, where Crystal halted amidst some ruined, crushed fruits and vegetables. Harvey joined him and waited awkwardly while Crystal paced about, mumbling to himself before turning and facing St Agatha's.

'Look,' said Harvey. 'I understand. Really. I was a hospital chaplain once.'

Crystal looked away.

'You have voices, don't you?'

'No.'

'Well, okay, so you don't have voices. It wouldn't matter to me if you did.'

Crystal softened a little.

'Okay,' Harvey told him. 'You're right. I was beginning to sound like a social worker. And you've had enough of them, right?'

Crystal felt more at ease. He scratched about in his pockets, feeling for a nub. But he only found threads of tobacco that caught under his long, foul fingernails.

'Could you buy us some fags?' he asked. 'I've not had a proper smoke for ages.'

Harvey's dimples deepened with his reluctant smile. He hesitated at first, since he had little money. But if everything went to plan at the jewellery quarter that would soon change. He dug into his trouser pocket and handed him the change left over from the ten pound note. How could he refuse Crystal? There was something magnetic about him.

'I'll wait here,' Harvey told him and watched Crystal set off for the newsagents at the corner of Market Square. The noises of the market place filled the air. Amidst the rotting produce that gathered where the last of the stalls ran beneath a line of trees, Harvey reminisced about his days as a young hospital chaplain at Winson Hall Mental Hospital in Derbyshire before he was relocated to Southwick Archdiocese. Some of the more colourful sequences caught up in the hooks of his mind: the man who casually cut open his neck and asked Harvey to guide his razor, the clarinettist who played jazz along the dark corridor, patients giving blowjobs for a single cigarette. And then in a flash the face of a man, on a blood-soaked mattress, his wrists chopped, a note to his wife shaking in his fist and crying out weaker and weaker, 'I don't want to die!' It was just that he didn't want to live. Then the silly face of a patient who had set fire to himself, climbed into the big cat enclosure of the local zoo, thrown himself from a block of flats and still survived, only to choke on a tuna sandwich. The mad, bad and the sad flooded in. Now, a whole new breed of memories rushed in on the back of his chaplaincy work in a variety of hospitals. But he tried to not think about this. Not after what had happened.

When Crystal returned, breaking into the cigarettes, Harvey

wanted to keep him at arm's length but at the same time draw him close and offer him some kind of friendship.

'Thanks for the fags,' Crystal said, lighting up, happy to have a clean cigarette to place on his blistered lip.

'That's okay.' Harvey was looking around the market, still expecting the journalist to pester him at any moment. But there was no one that fitted the bill. At least, he couldn't see anyone. Just a usual market crowd. 'You've still got some change left over?'

'Yeah,' said Crystal, jangling the few coins in the palm of his hand.

'How about a cup of tea?'

'Good idea.'

They moved to a part of the market that was free of stalls and where benches faced a white obelisk war memorial. Pigeons flapped away from Crystal's large feet and landed again, feeding on bits of bread that a child was shaking awkwardly from its fist. Normally, Crystal would have stopped and played with the pigeons. He often spent hours amongst them. They always came, his friends, the pigeons. They asked no questions. They didn't judge him by his clothes. Nor whisper behind his back. He was whole before their eyes, like any other man of Templeford. He would tut and beckon them. And they would flock willingly to his thick fingers, circling down from St Agatha's, or across from the shit-spattered obelisk. They would peck him, touch him briefly. When he felt their beaks tapping his flesh, and saw their iridescent necks trembling and close, he felt less lonely. But not today. He cut through them.

'I don't want sympathy, you know,' he said, the trail of words flung back at Harvey, the fag half burnt, dangling from his lip.

Harvey picked his way through the pigeons.

'Don't worry,' he said. 'You won't get it.'

Harvey thought that a no-nonsense approach was best with a character like Crystal. He was mad. So what? It was best not to make so much of it. He couldn't help feeling for him, though. After all, who cared about the mad? They were invisible, often homeless. Besides, he might hide in such company. After all that had happened to him, bedlam could give him the cover he needed to pass unobserved. All he needed to do was let his stubble grow a little longer, talk strangely or not at all, and dress a little incongruously, if he was not doing that already. Then he would more than likely disappear from view.

Harvey followed Crystal, a smile of satisfaction crossing his lips for the first time in days. Perhaps he was onto something with this idea of pretending to be mad. The pigeons lifted into the air, bellies full, circling low to the ground, eyes for more bread. Stopping suddenly, Crystal turned, drew on his fag and appeared to wait for Harvey to catch him up, before turning and walking on. Harvey was pleased with this gesture. He felt a little less isolated. Perhaps Crystal felt the same. All those years with just pigeons to get close to. And now from nowhere, a companion who did not mock him, sneer, or beat him up. He bowed his head, sucked smoke along the roof of his mouth and farted.

'That's all right, then,' he said, puzzling Harvey by the delay. 'Sympathy is a killer.'

'How about that place?' asked Harvey, pointing to a coffee shop.

Crystal shook his head.

'They won't serve me in there,' he said. 'We'll have to go to Greasy Joe's.'

Harvey didn't like the sound of the place but shrugged. Greasy Joe's was down by the Chinese takeaway and across from an adult magazine shop. Crystal pointed it out and smiled.

Still Harvey thought his smile was not quite right. There was something missing.

'Here we are,' Crystal said, peering through the misted windows to see if it was fairly empty. He did not like crowded tearooms. Inside, there were a few market traders, but mostly beggars and idlers, taking their time draining their oily cups. Most were smoking. Flattened fag-ends littered the cheap black-and-white tiling. Greasy Joe's. Nothing special. Nothing to it. Grime mounting and old food like gum in the cracks of benchlike tables.

Harvey's eyes began to sting as soon as he entered the shop. He hated smoking, but he would suffer it. Crystal had already made his way up to the counter since there was no queue. Harvey stood behind him, his hands stuffed into his pockets. He felt out of place. He sensed that the other customers had spotted that he was different to them. It made him feel all the more eager to change his clothing. Nothing purple. Nothing black. He twiddled his garnet ring and wondered how much he might get for it. Enough perhaps to seek out Montgomery? If he did finally choose to go south, that is. Just then Crystal pushed a steaming cup of tea into his hands. A cup of hot tea. Harvey licked his lips. I'll sell the ring first, he told himself, following Crystal to a table. The watch could wait. And the gold cross and chain.

As Harvey sat down he experienced a sudden burst of relief and thankfulness. The reporter had lost the trail and might lose it completely if Harvey chose to join bedlam. Here he was with his hot cup of tea, without the kind of hassle he had endured for the last few days. He had some company, although admittedly of a poor quality. Not a friend he would choose, of course. But a friend all the same. And he couldn't be too fussy. After all, he had no one in the world looking out for him. No family, nothing. But then again Harvey wondered if this wasn't a blessing. After all, he had no family to shame, to let down, to make angry. Crystal would have to do for now, for today. And perhaps for tomorrow, thought Harvey. He was glad to see his companion enjoying his tea and looking less distracted or suspicious. He was almost normal, Harvey thought. He was much less preoccupied than earlier on. He was like anyone else now, lighting a cigarette, playing with the sugar bowl, supping his tea.

'I'll sell this ring,' Harvey told him. Crystal looked up, nodded, and began to slurp at his cup. 'I'll leave the watch for now.' Crystal nodded again and drew deeply on his cigarette. Harvey noticed how the sleeve of his shirt had turned grubby. He covered it with the sleeve of his coat. The button of his shirt had opened at his neck, revealing his gold cross and chain. He did it up. He didn't want to tempt anyone to mug him for it.

Harvey's eyes grew tired and red in the smoke of Greasy Joe's. He could easily have cried to clear them, since he felt emotionally raw. The feeling had been building up inside him for days. It made him tense and churned his stomach. But Greasy Joe's was not the place for it. Maybe he would get a chance later to find some relief. Crystal looked blankly at Harvey's slightly trembling hands, bulb light dancing in the garnet of his ring. He slid the packet of cigarettes across the table and knocked Harvey's elbow.

Harvey looked down, shook his head.

'I don't smoke,' he told him, coughing, shaking out a single tear from his eye. It fell into the sugar bowl and welded a few granules together.

Harvey was thinking how things had changed since the heady days on Caldey Island. Everything had seemed perfect then. He had been staying at the monastery. Olwyn was at the guest house, taking a break from Tenby, where she ran a craft shop with the help of her mother. Day by day, Harvey and

Olwyn had exchanged glances on the farm track leading to the lighthouse and cliffs, in the gardens surrounding the monastery, and even down at the old farm, where the leaning steeple of St Illtud's became a warning finger to their growing interest in one another. Yet Olwyn was not allowed to enter the monastery. Only male visitors could walk its cloister. She was excluded. And when she did meet him, it was always in silence. He would nod or lift his hand, and sometimes smile the kind of smile that forms with meditation and prayer. A kind of benevolent grin.

Harvey recalled the day that silence was broken, and as he did so he began to slip from Crystal's company, from the café, from Templeford. And he was there, on Caldey, with the sea breeze knocking into his hair, salt on his lip, sand sifting between his bare toes. He had left his sandals on a wedge of concrete used to take boats down to the water, and walked slowly along the beach chanting the *Salve Regina*. Further along, halfway up the dark cliffs, he saw a strange, bobbing light, and was drawn to it. Like an oversize firefly, it descended slowly. It was Olwyn climbing down from the old quarry, down from a ledge and cave where, thousands of years ago, Neanderthals sheltered against the elements. The occasional moonlight with the passing of clouds was not enough to guide her path. She had to stop several times and light her way carefully over the rocks. Harvey approached the light, at peace in himself, his chanted prayer coming to a close. Walking alongside the water's edge, marvelling at the phosphorescent glow of waves breaking, he felt the retreat was doing him good.

The intense loneliness he had been feeling back at his parish had loosened its grip on him. He felt stronger, refreshed, less depressed. As usual the monks had been kind. Away from the constant pressures of parish life, he began to forget why he had ever doubted his ministry. True, his mother's death had robbed his vocation of its former spark. But he was determined to overcome such feelings. With prayer and rest, his special calling to serve God would be restored. The fire would return to his head. His dog collar would reflect light more strongly. Now, beside the sea, he felt the part; all fisherman; a disciple of the Lord. Like so much scaffolding, the retreat on Caldey was keeping Harvey's priestly edifice intact. Somehow, the weather-beaten gargoyles, outjuts of his fears and self-doubts, stayed in place. As he moved through the sand towards the light of Olwyn's torch, he enjoyed the quietness, the rush of water, the licking wind, the riding moon.

Harvey was not expecting a woman behind the torch beam. He thought it might be Brother Dominic returning from one of his many archaeological digs. More than this, he was not expecting the woman he had greeted so many times. Out from behind the rocks she came, noiselessly jumping down onto the sand. Although she gave a cry of surprise, Harvey doubted its sincerity. From the height she had descended, with everything intermittently silver, she must have seen him from afar. Yet he did not want to spoil such play. Her torch lit his open shirt and jeans and made him shield his eyes. She dropped the beam and clicked the torch dead.

'You gave me quite a shock,' she lied, drawing strands of her long hair behind an ear, like combing sand to reveal an open, moonlit shell. Harvey smiled, but stood awkwardly, flicking his eyes at her long legs, at the folds of her tee shirt altering in the breeze. He wanted to engage her eyes, but could not do it.

'I saw the light,' he answered her. 'It's rather late to be out climbing.'

Harvey sensed that this woman, who had silently punctuated his retreat, was pleased to hear him speak.

'It's not dangerous,' she said. Then she crossed her arms. 'You're a priest, aren't you?'

Harvey laughed, his hands open, like a caught thief.

'It's that obvious?'

All week, he had been wearing jeans and a shirt in the hope of losing that clerical air.

But Olwyn did not expand on the issue of cloth.

'This is my favourite spot,' she told him. 'There's a cave up there. It's got bats. I don't go in. I just sit outside on a ledge and look at the waves and the lights of Tenby. It's very pretty.'

'I know. I've been up there,' nodded Harvey, jamming his hands into his pockets, feeling vulnerable all of a sudden. He struggled to build a conversation. His throat fell dry, and he felt silly. He sensed he was blushing and turned away, taking his hands out of his pockets, pulling at his lips and chin, and finally scratching the back of his neck. Meeting the woman he had not failed to notice, who had brought frequent acknowledgement made him very uncomfortable. And to have exchanged words with her. Not in daylight. Not in the company of others. But here, beneath a cathedral of rock, in the fickle spotlight of the moon.

'I'm Olwyn,' she said and moved past him and down towards the water's edge. She intended him to follow, which he did, though delayed, all schoolboy. His heart was pounding, as he expected it might. His belly was burning, as he thought it would. He kept his eyes on the prints she made in the sand, with a deep pang of attraction. It's just the circumstances, he coached himself, nothing more. His excitement was a primitive response to finding himself alone with a woman, on a beach, at night.

'I'm Harvey,' he shouted dryly after her, breaking up the weight of silence and then keeping up.

Olwyn did not answer. She walked into the ebb and flow of the tide, her ankles lost and revealed, and lost again as the water seethed away. Harvey watched as she avoided the more forceful waves which kept their form till the last before fading into a prolonged hiss. In and out of the water she went. He enjoyed watching her from a distance, standing off the wet sand, his hands in his pockets again. With her back to him, he felt he could look at her more closely but did not do so. She was all in the corner of his eye; a blur of womanhood. He sensed he had already been written off by Olwyn as yet another dried-up priest. He felt as if he was giving off a peculiar odour, a priestly smell. Even in mainstream clothing, the smell went with him.

'I'm on retreat,' he said. 'How about you?'

They stood apart, as if fearful. Harvey had his hands behind his back, surveying his own thoughts of what to say next, how to proceed, how to unhook himself from excitement and retire unscathed to the monastery. Though it was a warm night, his teeth chattered delicately like the tinkle of china.

'Oh, I'm taking a break,' she said. 'Nothing special. I've been coming to the island since I was a child. The guest house up there is like a second home.'

'You live nearby?'

'Tenby. With my mother.'

Harvey nodded at the waves and stole a quick look at Olwyn. But he didn't really look at her. He had the lightest, afterburn image of her printed on the paper of his mind. Yet it was enough. He didn't have the nerve to study her for details. She was a shadow, a brush of charcoal, a fingerprint of all that Harvey found exciting.

'I have a shop,' she added. 'You know, a craft shop. I sell stuff from the monk's perfumery among other things like pottery, carvings and paintings. I travel all across the country, buying stock.'

Harvey had been to the perfumery. It looked like a huge corrugated bomb shelter, complementing the various World War II amphibious craft left dotted around the island.

While Harvey looked out at Tenby, imagining what the

65

craft shop was like and where it was exactly, Olwyn was looking at him. He knew she was looking, but he did not want to interrupt her gaze. He was enjoying it more than he should. She was thinking how grey his hair was. How he was old before his time, because she guessed he was in his late thirties at most. At first inspection, she thought he was not her sort at all. But then again, there was play in his face, in his dimples. He was, she decided, attractive in an awkward kind of way. His eyes seemed almost to lose themselves, but battled their way out, finally demanding attention. And she had seen, in daylight, how sharply blue they were, almost incandescent. His skin seemed heavy, like leather, but not in texture, nor deeply lined; heavy with his own and other people's suffering. He was not well-built like the men of Tenby. He was neither tall nor small. Yet he was firm, she judged, like a fish; not yet softened up like so many priests at the hands of indulgent housekeepers. Most of all, she liked his forearms, which looked lean and strong. And his bottom was small and tidy. It did not sag with too much pudding, nor disappear into his back.

Harvey appreciated Olwyn's company, talking with her about the island in general, about the storm which had been forecasted, about the difficulty that the island boat faced in getting across from Tenby in such weather. Olwyn seemed to know a lot about the sea and seamanship. Walking with her made Harvey feel normal, like any other guy, not set apart. And he felt good about himself. He had been continent. He hadn't embarrassed himself with any silliness or blurted out proposals. As they walked back towards the jetty, he was cool and contained like a mussel in its shell. Now he could return triumphantly to the monastery, having shared such a pleasant chat. There was no confusion, no terrible doubting about his vocation. Though he sensed that Olwyn liked him, he did not feel any deeper roots to her looks. He had been with a woman, alone, and survived again. To give up everything and follow the Lord was what he had chosen, and he knew that he would always have to battle with his appetite. I am a priest like Melchisedech of old. With such insulating thoughts, it came as a shock when Olwyn stopped dead in her tracks and asked whether he found being a priest intolerably lonely.

'Er,' he hesitated. He wanted to say no. But he didn't. 'Yes,' he told her.

But no sooner had he said it, than he drew the comment back into line. 'We're all lonely, don't you think? Most of the time? Even with company? It's like we're all orphans in space.' He looked up at the stars between the veils of silvered cloud.

Olwyn agreed with him but chose not to speak. Her not responding challenged Harvey to say more about his particular loneliness. This made him feel increasingly uncomfortable, especially since he hardly knew the woman at his side. He was surprised at how quickly she seemed to take a personal interest in him. And how quickly she had poked him in a tender spot. The light chit-chat hadn't lasted long. But Harvey did not wish to embellish his answer. He knew he was lonely, but he had no desire to keep going over that ground. He had lost count of the hours he had spent mulling over his sense of isolation, of being different from everyone else, of being disabled in some strange way. His loneliness was like white noise that was with him always. So he had learned to stop thinking about it, put it to the back of his mind. In time with such thoughts, he kept pushing his hair back over his scalp; first one hand, then the other, alternating his unease.

Olwyn maintained her silence. She left him no words to hide among or kick like sand over what had been revealed: his vulnerable, lonely heart. And when he finally reached the jetty and pulled on his sandals, he made the comment he feared he would make, and which set him on a painful walk back to his monastic cell.

'Just because I'm a priest,' he said, 'doesn't mean I can't express affection. I can't marry, of course. But I can – '

'Express affection.'

'Yes. Exactly.'

Olwyn said no more for a while. Harvey's words about loneliness seemed to come to a full stop. After a while, she changed the subject, lagging slightly behind Harvey as they ambled up the jetty and onto the path back to the village and monastery.

'Do you swim?' she asked.

Harvey wiped sweat bubbles from his nose and upper lip and slowed down even more, in deep thought.

'Of course. Yes, I – '

'Well, why don't you join me over at Sandy Cove tomorrow afternoon? Say half past one? I could use some company.'

Harvey took a long time thinking about this request. But there was a big enough hole in his Catholic sieve, and the idea avoided censure. Just where the path forked, leading off to the guest house, he wiped more sweat from his head and took the plunge.

'I'll have to borrow an outfit. So I can't say for definite.'

'Okay. Well, I might see you tomorrow, then. Bye,' she said, giving the air that if he came, he came; if not, then it did not matter.

As Olwyn signed off, she took the left fork, heading behind the dunes and back towards the cliff. She didn't turn her head. Harvey watched her go before returning to the cool, white monastery. On the way, he chewed the cud over what had been said between them, what he meant, what she implied, and how best to proceed. With sweat forming a sheet of moisture across his hot face, he began to see the danger of a swim. There would be no innocent swim. There would be something else motivating him. The thought sent him hot and cold. It was asking for trouble. He knew you didn't walk around a sweetshop unless you wanted a sweet. But as Harvey approached the lit grotto of the Virgin, he found a train of thought that would let him put his head into the lion's mouth: she knows I am unobtainable. It is a swim. There is nothing in a swim. It is a swim, nothing more.

And that is all it was: a swim. Except that it rained and made the occasion memorable. Harvey floated on his back, with the black, ill-shaped trunks he had borrowed from the overweight Abbot. They were puffed up like a bladder. The rain pitted the swollen, dark green water to the delight of Olwyn who, with her hair tied back, moved like a frog in small circles. Beyond two bags that kept their clothes dry, the high sandy bank of the deserted cove rose up to meet the bleak sky. A wonderful, ominous orangey light filled the scene.

Every now and then, Harvey looked at Olwyn: a tint of blue around each segment of lip, gooseberry eyes, slightly flat but attractive nose, pale skin, dark lashes which stuck together unevenly in the salt water. But what caught his eye each time she rose from the water was the thin white scar, whiter than her skin, that divided her chest. He wondered why she did not wear a full costume instead of the pink bikini she had on. Why did she choose to show off her scar? Especially since she was so conscious of it. She put her arm across her ribs when Harvey seemed to be looking at it. But Harvey did not account for Olwyn's tenacity. Though the mark distressed her and had sent several boyfriends back into their undergarments, she was determined to include it in her life, and not hide it away like some dirty little secret. Harvey also thought the best policy was to include it.

'Sorry, I can't help noticing the scar on your chest. Was it from an operation?'

'Yes,' she said rather snappily. 'Hole in the heart.' She sank back in the water till just her head bobbed above it, veiled in rain.

'Right. Right. Nasty, huh? But they did a neat job, if you don't mind me saying. You can hardly see it.' Trying to make light of the issue, Harvey gave a rallying cry and dived beneath the waves. When he surfaced, Olwyn was closer. Harvey lay face upwards, eyes closed, floating, a sperm of water lifting from his mouth and falling back onto his mask-like face. Olwyn laughed at him, appreciating the distraction. He then performed a handstand, complete with puffed-out trunks.

He was fun, she decided. At least he was more fun than the priests she had met before. And those blue eyes of his, stung by salt, looked lively. Her scar did not seem to alter Harvey's attitude towards her. He seemed constant, true. It left her wondering if she would ever meet someone like Harvey; someone who did not stare at her chest and wince. At first, men were often attracted to her. She was thirty, plain, but had that twist of mischief in her face that tipped the balance in her favour. And she guessed Harvey liked her a lot. But she knew that he was beyond reach. He was lost in the embrace of that big, fat Holy Mother, the Church, with her nipple rammed into his mouth, preventing him from speaking to other girls.

But he was good company. And that was fine, she decided, kicking her frog's legs, the rain pattering her shoulder.

'Why did you become a priest?' she asked after swimming another circle around him. He pulled a face, sending commas into his cheeks, before sinking beneath the water and surfacing nearby. She looked steadily at his dripping nose and plastered-down hair. He was not old, despite the grey hair. She studied him, wondering whether there was any rebellion behind the serious look that he often gave, and was giving now. What was left of Harvey behind the dog collar? Was he just a good dog? He stood higher in the water, wiping his eyes, mouth and chin, sniffing briefly.

'I get asked that all the time,' he said, pushing his hair backwards, looking directly, for the first time it seemed, into Olwyn's eyes; not just around the whites of her eyes, or the green spokes of iris, but right into the intimate little black dots. 'It's difficult to explain. The idea just grew on me, I guess. It seemed a natural evolution from being an altarboy.' He laughed.

Olwyn smiled and lay back in the water, blinking at the rain. After a few moments' silence, she spoke again.

'Did you know what you were giving up?'

'Yes and no. I mean, I suppose so,' he said. 'When I was at Holtham College, I knew I wanted to be ordained. So I went on to seminary. Afterwards, I had some doubts, of course, from time to time. You know, when you see somebody you like and think, what if I had a family? Stuff like that.'

'You were never tempted, you know?'

'Oh, yes, quite often. Sometimes I felt like I was keeping all those kinds of emotions in a tin can. But one found ways of relieving the tension. When I first went to work in a parish on my own, that was the worst time. I got lots of attention, and with nobody looking over my shoulder, well, I was sorely tempted. I suppose, it was then that I realised what I was giving up. I found weddings a bit of a trial. Strange as it sounds, priests generally find weddings more disturbing than funerals.'

Olwyn laughed, but then apologised.

Gradually, the rain gave over, sweeping inland from the Bristol Channel and bringing brighter weather. Gaps of sunlight broke through and altered the dark, ominous light brought by the rain. The swim was coming to a close. Both Harvey and Olwyn were getting cold, and the skin at the tips of their fingers had grown rippled with water.

'We can walk along the cliffs towards the lighthouse, if you like,' suggested Harvey, stepping from the water, holding the austere black trunks around his middle. Further back in the cove stood their bags like rocks. They made their way towards them. As they walked, Harvey kept looking down at Olwyn's long, slender legs dripping water onto the sand, and, above her legs, the fluorescent triangle of pink bikini. He felt he could look at her now. They had talked a good deal. They had swum together. Yet, although scanning her body closely, he felt in control. He convinced himself that it was fitting to enjoy the sight of her body, as he might a rare orchid. But seeing can be painful, and he had forgotten just how much. Goosepimpled, Olwyn quickly set about drying her legs and belly. Without intending to do so, this action nudged the triangle of her bikini downwards, revealing a little more of her flesh. It wasn't much, but sufficient for Harvey to struggle, to tremble, to shiver with self-doubt. He opened his mouth wide to release as noiselessly as possible a snarl of passion. But it was also a cry for completion. With towels wrapped around their waists, they dressed awkwardly, self-consciously, afraid the towels might fall away, hoping they might.

They climbed out of the cove, helping each other up the bank of sand that was as soft as snow, pulling at the clumps of dune grass. And along the cliff path they went, slowly, each carrying a damp roll of towel under an arm. As they walked, Olwyn spoke of the recent death of her father. He had run a fishing trip boat from Tenby harbour, taking tourists out to catch mackerel. He had a big black beard, flecked with ginger, and crow's-feet from squinting so much. She recalled how he had carried her as a child on his shoulders, and how she still wanted to look at the world from seven feet up. Now he had gone, vanished from sight, taking up a new life in old photographs. He had tried to rescue a boy who had fallen from the boat in a rough sea. Neither surfaced again. Her father left some money, which helped to keep the craft shop going. It had been struggling along for some years. Now Olwyn and her mother had been able to build up a better stock, and things were going well. They both lived above the shop in a cosy flat, with a view over the harbour. Her mother sometimes stood at the window, as if at any moment she would catch sight of a man with a big black beard, climbing the harbour steps.

'He used to help out with the Abbey's boats,' she told Harvey. 'That's why I like coming over here. He liked this place. I feel he's around sometimes, you know?'

'Have you any brothers or sisters?'

'No. It's hard to believe, being Catholic and everything.'

'Not at all, I'm the same,' said Harvey. 'You have your mother, though. Both my parents are dead.'

'I'm sorry,' Olwyn said quietly, laying a consoling hand at his elbow.

'I miss them a lot.'

As they walked on in silence, Harvey kept snatching a look at Olwyn. He had already grown rather fond of the flatness of her nose and the straightness of her lips. But it was somehow the absence of anything striking about her looks that excited Harvey. There was no hierarchy of features. He did not feel he had to edit her face to like it more: make good a nose, chin or brow; exaggerate the beauty of one trait to make good what was lacking elsewhere. Olwyn fell short of definition as such. She was quite beyond caricature. If Harvey's gaze was to rest anywhere, it was on her eyes. It seemed that what was absent from her face in general was a funnel to those gooseberry-ringed dots. And, having turned inland from the lighthouse, and walked down towards the monastery, it was with a last look into those dots that Harvey took leave of her. As he moved away past the old red fire engine that stood at the rear of the monastery, she stood still and watched him grow smaller, and disappear through a dark doorway.

The following day they met in the little Post Office, a low-roofed building which also served as a grocery and, in its back rooms, a public house for the islanders. At this time of year, it was busy with visitors. Harvey had just finished an hour of spiritual exercises in the monastery chapel and decided to send a few postcards to friends. In the doorway he met Olwyn, who had spent the morning with Brother Anselm at the perfumery, finalising orders of a new perfume for the craft shop, and wanted to check if any mail had been forwarded. They chatted away like old friends, and drew curious looks from some of the islanders. They all knew Olwyn through her father. He had brought supplies over from Tenby when bad weather kept the more fearful sailors indoors. But they also knew Harvey. As a callow seminarian, he had spent several summers helping the monks by serving tea and sandwiches to the tourists. They remembered how he had insisted upon wearing a cassock, even on hot days and when joining in the annual cricket match. Back then he had seemed oblivious to the island's womenfolk, and was considered stiff and haughty. Now he had filled out, looked more human and approachable. The general consensus was that the death of his parents had made him a less fireproof and altogether warmer person.

With the postcards sent and mailbox checked, Harvey invited Olwyn for a walk past the village green and school-house, to the enclosure behind St David's chapel, not far from the spot haunted by the Black Monk. This enclosure was strictly out of bounds to the general public, but Harvey no longer felt strongly for rules. Olwyn felt less sure about walking along the private paths that divided the woodland. But Harvey insisted that it would be fine. The tree-covered paths were lush with short, deeply green grass, that here and there clotted with dappled light. Various shrines to holy men and women littered the maze of shadowy paths, and had that timeless, still, almost forlorn feel to them. The privacy and quietness intensified the pitch of togetherness of Harvey and Olwyn. There was something exquisite about walking in a forbidden way through a space devoted to prayer and contemplation. It was a landscape of prohibition that might change fear into something sweeter, altogether delightful.

In the middle of the enclosure, where they could barely hear the distant fall of waves, they sat down on a stone bench before a grey figure of an unknown saint. His head looked down upon them. His chiselled lips were drawn inwards as if sad. A real, decayed flower had been placed in his outstretched hand. The holes for his eyes conveyed a life that was never there.

Although Harvey and Olwyn sat still for a long time, a pressure to speak mounted, and with that pressure, as yet hidden feelings of desire stirred. Harvey had experienced such potent silences many times before, mostly in the confessional box, where he used it to good effect, like a poultice on the soul. It never failed. And he sensed that same quality of silence was working on Olwyn, such that the string of words she held back behind those straight lips would eventually stream forth. But he did not see the fine trembling of her head. He kept brushing his jeans nervously, and fidgeting with the rolled-up sleeves of his sea-blue shirt.

'You are good to be with,' she said eventually, her breath coming a little hot, and staggering back into the cover of silence. Her words surprised her. Her head trembled more heavily. She knew that these words meant more, demanded more. Yet this simple declaration was already opening places in Harvey's heart that did not yet exist. Her words told him that there was ground he could move onto if he wanted to. He could begin to chase her now until she caught him. Yet her comment was also safe, leaving escape routes should he pursue her too wantonly. Her line was an opening gambit. She could retract into friendship. Or she could blow on the little fire that was burning at this very moment in Harvey's throat.

Harvey took what she said as if it were a little gift or present, which, in a way, it was.

'Thank you very much,' he said, smiling anxiously, aware of the play at hand, but struggling all the same. He kept flicking his gas-flame eyes around the wood, and twisting his feet meaninglessly into the mulch. He suddenly wished for the confessional grid to hide behind. That board of holes, which broke his features, that turned him into a shadow.

'It's been a long time since I've felt this relaxed in male company,' Olwyn admitted, averting her gaze as she spoke. She felt that the face on the statue looked a little shocked rather than sad. She felt a deep unease that the figure just might move, like one of those whitened street artists, and begin to alert the monks about what was happening, in their own backyard as it were.

The pressure to speak was now with Harvey, who snatched a look at Olwyn, with her legs outstretched and pale hands in her flowery lap.

'Well, that's good,' he said finally. 'Good. Very good.'

But Harvey winced as he made such a banal response.

'Yes, I – well, I find it difficult to relax in the company of – but you're different.'

Now Olwyn remained quiet. She wanted the fantasies swirling beneath her skull to enter the real world, the shadowy enclosure, near the monastery, on Caldey Island. She desired something muscular and wordless. Any guilt she felt by throwing coals on the fire growing in Harvey's throat was past hearing. A nagging lust, at once deemed ridiculous, monstrous, unwarranted, began to grow. As much as she looked at his grey hair, weighed up the seriousness of his mind, and thought her desire unwise, she saw something in his blue eyes and dimples.

'Yes,' he continued haltingly, 'you talk to me rather than my collar. You know, I feel I don't have to speak, I don't know – ' He wiped his face and shook his head. 'Look,' he began again, his hand gestures more forthright this time. 'Meeting you has been like drawing a deep breath for the first time in ages. You can't imagine what that feels like for me. I've been taking shallow, defensive breaths. Do you follow? My whole life has been a life of sipping air as if each sip is poisonous to my soul.'

Now uninvited, but feeling drawn, Olwyn began to reveal more about herself, her life, her dreams. As she did so, she sat upright and quite forgot the uncanny statue. It wasn't a confession. It was a display for Harvey of who she was, where she came from, and what she wanted; the things she had done and hoped to do. And Harvey listened intently, without interruption, looking now and then at Olwyn's walnut hair and green eyes. He wanted to hug her close. He wanted to touch the satin of her skirt. He wanted to feel the fine hairs on her legs bend gently against the pad of his finger. He wanted all this, but sensed it wasn't the right time.

Beneath the hood of trees, she told him of the men who had let her down, turned so hot and then so cold. She said how she used to turn the light out when she undressed so that they could not see the surgical mark and how she dreaded that they might feel what she stole from their eyes. And how all this left her feeling like every bone in her body was somehow out of joint. She got through, she said, by going out every night and collecting friends. It was as if her popularity was merely a symptom of loneliness. Yet, after her father's death, she calmed down and no longer felt desperately addicted to the company of other people, although she still felt lonely.

Her words were not lost on Harvey. He knew only too well the grip of loneliness and the attempt to escape it. He had seen loneliness deeply etched on the faces of fellow priests, desperate to play some golf together, or meet for a drink. He had felt the skin of his face tight with loneliness when visiting families in their homes. He knew how the black clothes and dog collar threw cold water on having a proper social life or even conversation. He detested the carefully edited talk of parishioners. And Harvey told Olwyn how his vocation became almost meaningless after the death of his parents. When Olwyn heard the tears in his throat on their way to his eyes, she wanted to grasp his hand and stroke it. But it was not the time.

'Harvey, Harvey,' Crystal insisted, the glow of cigarette intensifying as he drew in his breath.

'Harvey,' Crystal said again and suddenly Harvey saw the cigarette dangling from his strange companion's mouth and knew he was where he didn't want to be. The smoke from the dangling stick of filth irritated his eyes, and he rubbed them fiercely.

'Best get on,' Crystal insisted. 'Best get along to the jewellers, you know. Sort things out.'

'What? Oh God, yes, the jewellers.'

And out they went into the square, past St Agatha's to the jewellery quarter, Harvey slow, thinking of recent calamitous events like a dog chasing its tail. He had messed up so much. Not just his life, but the lives of Olwyn and others who looked up to him. And now Olwyn must be feeling lost too. What would she do with herself? What would become of her? Shouldn't he have made her happy, gone off with her and started a fresh life? She had betrayed him, but he could not blame her. He only blamed himself. He felt disgusted with his behaviour. His eyes welled up with the shame. He had been so shapeless after all, so damned shapeless. So much pride and fear. He had been running away from everything. He saw the mitre falling upon his head in slow motion, and a sick testicular ache moved upwards to his throat.

Before long Harvey and Crystal had reached the jewellery quarter. Harvey had been oblivious all the way. He had just stepped in Crystal's gumbooted footsteps. It wasn't so much a quarter as a single, rather narrow street, running south and following the railway line. Here were button, buckle and badge manufacturers, silversmiths and goldsmiths, electroplaters, die-sinkers, skilled and unskilled alike, taking a lunch break, wandering up and down, eating sandwiches or picking into bags of chips. It was too cold to sit about. And as always in this diamond-mounting, gem-setting part of the town, young couples flocked in to buy engagement and wedding rings at trade prices. Many would come from Hickley, Metchley, Stonehill and surrounding towns.

Crystal looked in at a window display, with its red cushion trays of signet rings, bracelets, solitaires and pendants. Between the gaps, he saw the jeweller, with a scowling, white-stubbled, red face. He was examining Crystal as if he were a cheap brass ring. As he did so, he pinched his fat, bottom lip, shook his head and slid out of view. Harvey had walked further on, staring into the brightly lit windows of more jewellers. Crystal caught up with him just as Harvey made a choice to try a rather run-down kind of place with a dusty, red linoleum floor, and tatty counters covered with fingerprints. Crystal stayed outside.

'Can I help?' asked a woman walking sideways out of her office.

'Well, yes, perhaps you can. I have a – '

Harvey began screwing his ring back and forth along his finger.

'I have a – '

The woman watched, dabbing an eyebrow, cool as gold.

'I'm having trouble getting it off,' Harvey told her.

The woman's brows lifted slightly. Harvey bent forward, chewing his lip, frowning with the effort, sucking in bits of air, testing how much pain he could take as the ring stuck at his blanched knuckle. He needed soap.

Respite came with a lick of his tongue. The ring eventually loosened and popped into his hand.

Affording a yawn, the woman held her neck between perfect lilac nails and asked if Harvey knew the strange man looking in through the window. Harvey looked round over his shoulder and shook his head. 'Never seen him before,' he said. He wondered if Crystal would pick up on this. Crystal seemed to be staring up at the sky. He looked fearful. With lips parted and jaw hanging loose, he wore the look of a man who was watching a plane about to crash. The woman twisted her shoulder away from the strange figure of Crystal.

'There,' said Harvey, pushing the ring over the sticky glass surface.

The woman took it as if it had come from a corpse, doubting its worth almost immediately with a curt shrug of her brow, a slow sniff and a rolling of her head from one side to the other. After some time, she puckered her lips, compressed the features of her face and laid the ring back on the counter.

'How much did you want for it?' she asked him with a price already settled in her mind.

Harvey stalled, dipped his head, scratched his grey nascent beard.

'How much will you give me?'

It was that question again. The one she heard day in, day out. She was in no mood for this.

'You tell me how much you wanted.' She looked uninterested, yawning again, and patting her mouth.

'Well, I don't know,' Harvey battled on, reddening a little under what he perceived to be a critical gaze. He felt he was being interrogated by eyes. He sensed her gaze slipping its fingers around his grime-laden collar. There was disgust. She picked up the ring again, knocked it about in the palm of her hand, and shook her head contemptuously.

'Only nine carat,' she told him.

Harvey was burning now. Behind her resolute mouth a smirk was breeding.

'And a garnet,' she objected, giving Harvey a cutting glance that made him want to shrink away like a snail. 'So?' she asked.

'Er.'

'Look,' she said, her tone softening, knowing she had won. 'It isn't worth a fat deal now, is it? I can only give you the scrap price, okay?'

Harvey pushed his grey hair back over his scalp and held his neck. Scrap? He felt pressured by the silence which fell on him. He would have to make a decision. Tortured by the prickly heat, desperate for money in his pocket, he bit his lip.

'How much will I get?'

'I'll weigh it,' she told him with such a light, feathery voice, caressing the air. Harvey watched and hoped. The ring tinkled lightly on the scale.

'Well, that is deceptive,' she lied. 'Who would have thought it was that heavy? Well I never.'

That was enough of a spark for Harvey. His face lit up. Down went the bait.

'Thirty pounds,' the woman told him. 'That's not so bad, is it?'

Harvey swallowed. He looked out at Crystal. Crystal was still preoccupied with the sky.

'Do you want to sell it?'

'Yes, fine. Yes, thank you. Thank you.'

Even before Harvey left the shop with the money curled up in his hand he felt guilty. He touched the shiny patch of skin where the ring had sat and shook his head. But beggars can't be choosers, he told himself. He needed cash. How else could he survive? And he knew that before long he would have to sell the watch and cross and chain. Thirty pounds was hardly enough. But he tried not to think about this. Just like he was trying to forget that Christmas was coming. The cruellest season, where it would be an achievement to get through with a full belly and a roof over his head. That was aim enough. After that, who could say? But Harvey's optimism was frail.

'Walk quickly,' Crystal said suddenly as they headed off in the direction of the market again.

'What?'

But Crystal simply grabbed his arm and quick-marched Harvey across the road. Harvey tried to look back over his shoulder while at the same time keeping upright.

'Don't look, for Christ's sake!' Crystal warned him. 'Just keep walking.'

'Is somebody after you?'

'Just keep walking.'

'But there's no one there,' Harvey assured him, jamming the few crisp notes into his coat pocket.

'That doesn't mean anything.'

People stopped and stared as the pair of them tumbled along the pavement at a rate of knots, hardly drawing a breath between them, escaping some nightmare or other.

Crystal's grip was even tighter than when Harvey had been prevented from catching his train.

'What the hell's wrong?' he blustered. 'What's going on?'

'Move, move. You don't want to know.'

'Yes I do.'

'No you don't. Believe me.'

Only when they reached the market did Crystal slow down and let go of Harvey's arm. Then gradually he appeared less agitated. He stood silent for some time before hitching up his trousers and tightening the string around them. He was panting and licking his blistered lip. It was dark now, and here and there blue, red and green Christmas lights adorned the market stalls. Crystal took a fag from somewhere and lit up, looking nervously over his shoulder just to be safe.

'They've gone,' he said, sucking the little burning tip under his nose.

Happy now that there was nothing lurking among the stragglers who came late to the market for the bargains, he blew smoke downwards, towards the cobbles. Harvey just stood dumbfounded in his own deepening, bulb-cast shadow.

'What was all that about?' he asked finally.

For a while Crystal just carried on sucking at his fag, looking at him as if he wasn't to be trusted.

'Nothing. You don't want to know.' Smoke trickled out between his rough teeth.

'But – '

'Leave it,' Crystal told him, raising the flat of his hand. 'Just leave it. Let's get what we came here for.'

And so they shopped with the dregs of shoppers, not speaking except to pass judgement on the few racks of shirts and trousers that traders had begun to pack up into their trailers and vans. Moving from stall to stall, the pair of them drew contemptuous glances. The market traders were dropping prices of vegetables and other corruptible foods. Crystal examined some hats, poking at the sleep that appeared constantly in the corners of his eyes.

The little money Harvey had would not stretch far. He could not afford to be fussy. He was thinking about buying warehouse or second-hand stuff. He hung the cheapest jeans against his hip, and examined the least fashionable jumpers. As he shopped he still wondered what had got into Crystal. What did he imagine was after him? What was he so afraid of? Harvey guessed there was nothing to it. Some paranoia, no doubt. Whatever it was, it kept the sweat balling up on Crystal's lip. That gave the measure of his fear. And in this atmosphere, Harvey could not help but worry about him. And worry about himself.

5

'There is no truth whatsoever in the *Evening Post*'s report,' Kilgarriff said, stepping from the doorway into a pit of reporters and photographers crunching the gravel. Kilgarriff's black hair flapped in the blustering wind that always seemed to plague that side of the house. Yet his knife-sharp trousers kept their shape. From upstairs, Barry Tourville kept watch, blinking at the flashlight. Above, the sky looked ominous and fruited for a storm. He kept just one half of his face peering out from behind the expensive curtains. He had no wish to be at Kilgarriff's side. Besides, Kilgarriff was a past master at ripping up paper stories. The muckrakers had little muck; nothing, at least, with the sticking power of the hidden truth.

'Let me tell you something,' Kilgarriff opened, candle-wax sincerity dripping. 'Bishop Harvey is a wonderful bishop. He has had a most difficult year. He has worked tirelessly for the good of his parishioners and the faithful of this, the Archdiocese of Southwick. It is regrettable, of course, that he has been poorly, yet he assures me that, given adequate time to rest and recover his strength, he will take up his position as Auxiliary Bishop. Now – '

'What's he doing in Templeford?'

Kilgarriff smiled.

'Passing through. Passing through. He is on his way to one of our retreat houses.'

'Is he an alcoholic?'

'Definitely not.'

'Is there a woman involved?'

'No, of course not.'

'Can you name the retreat house, Your Grace?' asked another, stroking at pockmarks in his cheek.

'Yes, but I'm not about to tell you. Do you think for one minute I want him hounded? He needs rest. Rest he shall have. Now, gentlemen, if you don't mind – I have much to do.'

When Kilgarriff had shaken off the paper men, Tourville descended and met him as he was coming back inside. Kilgarriff stopped briefly on the doorstep, lit up one of his cigarettes, and almost finished it in one long, anxious drag. When he saw Tourville he shrugged and loosened his frown.

'Get the car out, Robert,' he said. 'I don't want us to be late. It's gone six.'

Tourville scowled as Kilgarriff passed by.

The Cambridge stood in what used to be the old stables, bleeding oil into hoof-pocked dirt, kicked up by the old mare that once belonged to Kilgarriff's predecessor Archbishop Jordan. But the mare had died. Tourville had no complaints. He was allergic to horses. He was only too glad, as he opened the doors, and pulled the light switch, to see a motor car. It did not bolt. It had no life, except the twist of a wrist he gave it, the play of his feet on the pedals. He opened its door, smelt the leather gladly, and turned the key. The engine jolted and lit the back of the house with its headlights. The wheels spun, cuffed the dirt and took the car to the front and Kilgarriff.

Tourville always drove. Kilgarriff disliked driving. He could never relax with it. It was bad enough being a passenger. The whole business of driving, especially on motorways, gave him headaches. In the leathery darkness he put on the seat belt, and said nothing to Tourville as the car pulled out onto the main road and descended into Burnt Green, gaining speed with the drop, and quickly moving along the main road out into the countryside, the full beam searing trees. They sped along the motorway for some miles, Kilgarriff's heart racing a little as always, particularly as the car approached the backs of other cars, but his head stayed clear. For once he did not drive from the back seat. When finally they reached Hickley, Tourville slowed down.

There was nothing startling about Hickley, apart from its huge hospital, St Philomena's. It had little history otherwise, a bland set of shops and public houses. In fact, it was a fill-up and drive-on place. But it had lots of people living out unspectacular lives. It also had one of the biggest Catholic parishes in Southwick. The Church of St Patrick was one of Hickley's high spots. It was a large hexagonal building with a double-pronged spire that the local drug addicts called Double Rush. The figure of Christ stood pinned to one of the concrete walls. He appeared unhappy overlooking such an average place, filled with average people. His face seemed unimpressed. His outstretched arms almost said 'Where the hell is this?' Tourville liked to think the figure was remonstrating with the Russian architect who had designed the building.

He swung the car into a space in the church car park and walked towards the presbytery, a modest end terrace. Kilgarriff squeezed a button on his watch and a light came on.

'I hope Macmillan has sorted everything out.'

'I'm sure everything's fine,' Tourville reassured him. 'After all, he is the kind of chap to do what he is told.'

'Is that right?' Kilgarriff took a long cigarette from his breast pocket and lit up. 'A man we can put our trust in?'

'Certainly, Your Grace.' They got out just as the sacristan, John Molloy, left the Hall where the meeting was being held. He came over, head dipped, his one shoulder leading the other, trying to look as if he had not noticed who had arrived but failing miserably. His eyes were far too lively.

'Hello, Your Grace,' he began, his hand jumping to his chest. 'I didn't see you in the dark. The dark being so dark.'

The man's an idiot, thought Kilgarriff.

'Hello, James,' he boomed. 'Is Father Macmillan about?'

Molloy felt slighted to the quick at being misnamed, but did not have the courage to contradict His Grace.

'If you would follow me.'

Although Molloy had not taken vows, he always wore a black cassock and mockingly was known in the parish as Father John. He was so proud of his role that he rarely washed his cassock, as the wax droppings and layers of dandruff testified. He was a man for candles. He was always in the sacristy, trimming them, stacking them like dynamite into drawers, running his fingers across them lovingly.

Wax and incense were smells that Molloy had widened his nostrils for all these years. He was at home with them. So long as he pottered around the sacristy or down the aisle of St Patrick's, impaling candles on spikes, sweeping the confessional boxes, tidying the hymnals, he felt safe, protected. He felt he might just live forever. Sometimes he would take out the brightest chasubles and try them on and stand before the long sacristy mirror transformed, glittering. At those times, he did not care to notice the flaking skin of his forehead, the ginger hairs poking from his nostrils, the roundness of his back. He was beautiful. He was a butterfly. He was Father John.

Within the presbytery, Macmillan was watching television, his feet up and a corncob pipe in his hands. As Kilgarriff entered he stopped picking his lip and jumped up. He jumped up so quickly that it was hard to believe he had just been seated. He moved like a chicken that had lost its head.

'Your Grace, Your Grace,' he cried. 'Sit down, please. Here, here, here. It's great that you have come. And Barry as well.

How's Barry? You're well, I take it? Good. That's great, really great. Now does anyone want a drink?'

Kilgarriff was being shepherded into a large, bloated chair in the far corner of the room. Tourville winced. Macmillan's bleep went off. He looked deep into it, scratched his head, then popped it back in his pocket. He hated being hospital chaplain. It depressed him. Although the hospital was literally across the road, he tried to keep away from it as much as possible.

'Tea? Coffee? John, would you put the kettle on?' But Kilgarriff shook his head.

'I'm in no mood for refreshment,' he said. His face chilled Macmillan.

Kilgarriff was up on his feet now. He walked across the room, his square jaw raised, lips rolled up, a finger trailing along the dusty top of the television set. He frowned deeply and switched it off. There on the television was a framed photograph of Harvey receiving a large cheque to help build the Youth Club. Kilgarriff simply turned the frame around to face the other way.

'Not even an orange juice?' Macmillan persisted. Kilgarriff just pulled down his eyes from under the lid of brow.

'Now, she spoke to you, didn't she?'

'Yes, that's right. She came to the presbytery and wanted to know where Harvey had gone. She said she had to get in touch with him urgently. She had something important to tell him. But I told her that he had disappeared.'

'She hasn't been back?'

'No.'

'And she won't go selling her story to the press?'

'I doubt that very much, Your Grace. Trust me, I don't think we'll see any more of her.'

'Are you sure she won't go blabbing?'

'I don't think she will.'

'And her house?'

'The diocesan solicitors purchased it before it went on the market. They did a deal with the estate agent.'

Kilgarrifff looked thoughtful.

'Will you make sure,' he said finally, 'nothing is left to remind me of my greatest mistake? They've bricked everything up, I hope?'

'Yes, the builders were in yesterday. They'll do the plastering tomorrow.'

Kilgarriff looked harshly at the parish priest.

'And we can rely on your discretion?'

'I'll remain as quiet as a gargoyle.' As he said this, Macmillan happened to be looking across at Tourville's high blank forehead and beaky mouth, and considered that he would fit that particular role better than him. Tourville delivered one of his camp shrugs and looked unimpressed. Now Macmillan desired a friendlier footing to his conversation with the Archbishop, but he sensed that Kilgarriff was in no mood for idle chat. Macmillan found the weight of silence unbearable. He circled the room, closing curtains, folding a newspaper sprawled next to his chair, snapping the lid back onto his tobacco tin. Tourville looked at his watch and caught Kilgarriff's eye. Kilgarriff looked at his watch. Macmillan looked up at the clock on the wall.

'Right, are we ready?' Tourville asked.

Kilgarriff rubbed his hands.

'They're expecting an explanation. Let's give them one.'

Macmillan tucked his pipe into his black jacket and told Kilgarriff to expect a large crowd. Kilgarriff was not impressed but knew that a good turnout would help. Give them the message you want them to hear and send them into the world to disseminate it. Tourville led the way out of the presbytery with Molloy bringing up the rear, knocking some of the dandruff from his shoulder as he went.

At the Church Hall, Kilgarriff made his entrance, puffing up his chest with a long, deep breath and holding his ribs up like a bird cage in front of him. Then came Tourville and Macmillan. Tourville kept as far away as he could from the parish priest. The hall was dense with people, all eager to hear what the Archbishop had to say about recent rumours.

Kilgarriff raised the lines of his face. Confidence and optimism, he schooled himself. Up face, up. Face like a billboard. There. Long in the tooth, he sensed the room was full of gossips, word vultures. There would be plenty of messengers for the lies he was about to tell. His lies would spill like oil on troubled water. His lies would be repeated right across the Archdiocese. He smiled at everyone. As he reached the podium he affected a stumble to show everyone that he too was human. He stopped and chit-chatted with several people at the front of the hall. His hard jaw softened a little, yet the fierce creases in his trousers held firm.

Macmillan led His Grace to the podium, while those who had bothered to turn up and miss an evening's television settled down and whispered. Macmillan smiled at his parishioners, lifting his hand to one or two and bowing gently, or raising his brow in feigned surprise at somebody's presence. Plucking out a dark hair from his nostril, he pointed to the carafe of water and offered a glass to Kilgarriff.

Kilgarriff began his address with the sign of the cross, which the parishioners repeated as if all of them had lost something between their shoulders and head.

'First, let me welcome you all, and thank you for coming this evening,' he said. The whispering continued unabated, especially towards the back of the crowd. 'It is with great sadness that I speak to you this evening. As you know, Father Macmillan was kind enough to invite me over – I accepted without hesitation – the events over the last week or so being both upsetting and misrepresented in the press. Our newly appointed bishop, so much at home here at St Patrick's – always inspired by the good work carried out in this parish – has been subjected to the kind of allegations that the press usually direct at film and pop stars.'

Here, Tourville, who sat behind him, nodded his head in agreement and with feeling and thoughtfulness, little of which existed in him. Father Macmillan simply bowed his head and tried to think of happier and simpler times.

'And he has suffered so much at their hands and in a manner not befitting the high office of a Bishop of Our Holy Mother the Church, nor such a hard-working, sincere and dependable servant. Now, I know many of you have been making up your own minds, and no doubt listening to a lot of gossip about how Bishop Harvey came to leave your parish. But let me tell you that there has been a great deal of filthy lies surrounding recent events, and I would like to put the matter straight. Bishop Harvey has been ill for some time now. I fear that the stress of his appointment has drained his energy. And so, I have asked him to go and stay with The Little Sisters of Mercy, who as you know do great, great work for the sick clergy of our archdiocese.' There were several murmurs of sympathy for Bishop Harvey at this point.

'Now I think we should all pray for the bishop's speedy recovery.'

As Kilgarriff closed his eyes, a few parishioners automatically tumbled to their knees.

6

Forty miles away Harvey jumped from the tram, a bag under his arm, Crystal behind him. They had not spoken since leaving the market, and did not speak as they moved away from the tramlines, a gust of wind threatening to lift Crystal's new, felt slouch hat from his head and send it rolling back down the hill into Templeford. He placed a large hand upon it and set off homewards. He was less suspicious now. Harvey noticed that he no longer looked over his shoulder every minute. He no longer stared into the sky as if something were flying through it, descending upon him. And he stopped mumbling at his voices. Looking blankly ahead, he shifted along, a cigarette nub just a relic on his lip. He pinched it dead and flicked it away.

East Vale was busier than usual, with traffic following and overtaking the tram and people streaming in and out of late night shops or heading for the Fighting Cock or the Albion. And among the fruit and vegetable boxes set up outside a run-down supermarket, Christmas trees poked out, dull and sparse, their needles shaken down to the flagstones.

Crystal and Harvey took a left and then a short cut along a gully which ran behind the Working Men's Club. The gully used to be swollen with water from the reservoir, but now lay like a bloodless wound. Here and there the iron railings were missing, and dirt paths rose and fell, and litter stood out in the darkness.

Eventually they reached the hostel, having come out at the bottom of Pinckney Street. Crystal fumbled for his key in his oilskins, the wind still threatening to knock his hat off. The hostel door was left on the latch during daylight hours but locked at night. Harvey stood behind, huddling, feeling the cold, strands of his grey hair flipping back and forth. He grimaced and ground his teeth. Crystal dug his pockets with one hand and lay the other over his head to secure his hat. He swore as his collection of nubs fell from his pocket and were blown into the gutter. While he decided whether to pick them up or not, the front door of the hostel opened suddenly and a whole group of people stood in the narrow hallway, looking back at him.

'Ah,' cried a woman. 'Roland. Come on in, that's it. Out of the cold. And a friend with you. That's nice.' She turned to some other people, who were smiling identical, patronising smiles. 'Roland has been with us for five years now, haven't you, Roland? He wouldn't be happy anywhere else, would you, Roland?' Then finally she whispered to her guests how Roland was one of the more able residents.

Crystal took off his hat and moved quickly through the gauntlet of strangers to the stairway. He lowered his head as he passed. Harvey followed him, equally embarrassed, smiling a little perplexedly at the different faces. He guessed the woman who had spoken to Crystal was the landlady. He noticed that when she smiled, the eyelid over her left eye drooped and her shiny, hairless chin lifted at an unnatural angle as if she had at that very moment knotted a tie or rope around her neck. As he passed sideways, crablike, he did not fail to notice the lavishness of the landlady's accommodation. Through an open door he caught sight of an elegant glass chandelier, red carpet and huge flowery suite.

But Harvey did not hover. He did not care to watch the drooping eyelid. There was something about her that gave him the jitters. He guessed she was cruel. Whatever she was, he wanted to escape her presence, and climbed the stairs to Crystal's bedsit. As he climbed he felt her eyes like insects all over his back. He rose all the quicker for it. When he reached the landing, turned left, and moved past the toilet with its broken flush and shit-stained pan, he was glad to get behind Crystal's door.

'That's her,' Crystal moaned when Harvey entered. He pulled off his hat and skimmed it onto the sofa. 'Mrs Angel.'

'Mrs Angel!' Harvey laughed. 'Well, there are no wings sprouting!'

'Tell me about it,' said Crystal.

'Who were the others?'

Crystal grimaced. He took off his oilskin jacket and kicked his feet out of his shorn-off gumboots.

'Social workers. You can smell them a mile off. They come to check her out. First thing she does is give them tea and cakes down in her fancy room at the front. And they are so dumb. When she goes to the kitchen she presses this button on the wall. I've seen it. She presses it and listens in to what they say behind her back. Then when she returns she has the right amount of flannel to keep them happy.'

'Surely not,' doubted Harvey.

'I'm telling the truth,' Crystal told him.

Crystal was looking around the room now, searching for the bits of wood he always left lying about. But there weren't any. In the end he emptied some of his stuff from a cardboard box and shoved that into the grate.

'That will have to do for starters,' he said. Then, muttering to himself, he began to root behind the sofa and in the cubbyhole for something a little more substantial. Usually he was careful to gather twigs and other bits of wood during his travels. Mostly he got firewood from the waste ground down by the reservoir or where Roney Hill once stood. He certainly couldn't afford coal. And the pathetic electric fire Mrs Angel had supplied when he took the room had burned out long ago and not been replaced.

Harvey perched on the arm of the sofa and took out the clothes he had bought at the market. Not one of the garments was purple or black. He had carefully chosen a blue acrylic jumper, a yellow and green shirt, stonewashed jeans, grey socks and size eight training shoes. When he finished unpacking them, he picked up his holdall from next to the mattress and searched for his soap tub and razor. Behind him, Crystal's cardboard fuel bloomed into flames and died down. Crystal took the bottom drawer from the chest beside the door and emptied its contents onto the floor.

'This'll do for now.'

Harvey watched as a heap of tablets fell away and rolled out across the floor. Crystal had turned the drawer upside down. Now he was standing on it and pumping his weight downwards until, with a creak and then a loud crack, the thing gave way. Crystal's full weight hit the floorboards with a resounding crash which rattled the window. In the silence that followed, Harvey stared at the tablets finally coming to a standstill. Then he looked at Crystal, who began feeding the wood into the grate. At any moment, Harvey expected Mrs Angel and the social workers to come knocking on the door. But no one came. Perhaps she was on the intercom, that dreadful eyelid working like a third ear. Harvey guessed they had grown used to the noises of the mad.

Crystal said nothing. He just carried on building up the fire, and when the fire was raging, he gathered up most of the pills and threw them on top.

While Crystal stoked the fire, Harvey looked down at the mitre in his hands and laid it on one side, the light from the fire making the gold filigree sparkle on its bed of white silk. He remembered how proud he had been when it stood on his

95

head, making him tall, grand. But now he was just a nobody, bottom of the pile, useless fool. Now the mitre was a kind of dunce's cap. His numb fingers continued searching the bag for the soap tub and razor, but his mind was not in it. He broke off, took up the mitre again, and walked over to the window. I'll wash tomorrow, he told himself. I'll shave tomorrow. Tomorrow, a new day, a different set of clothes. Clothes change the person.

Crystal came to the window and opened it slightly before leaning out and bringing in his makeshift fridge.

'I'm hungry. How about you?' Crystal snuffled his nose clear, a lit fag-end dangling from his blister. He delved into the plastic carrier bag for the last of the sausages and bacon. Harvey shook his head. He remembered the lovely clean fridges that had always lit up his face. Now he was looking at his scruffy reflection in the bare dark glass window of a bedsit. Crystal disappeared into his cubbyhole kitchen, and soon his shadow was thrown out into the room by a flickering gas flame.

Quite forgetting himself, Harvey slowly placed the mitre on his head, and for a moment was back in front of the sacristy mirror at St Patrick's. He shuddered and pushed back those grey hairs that poked out untidily. Very quietly, he began talking to himself, like he did all those times before, on lonely nights, before love entered his life. 'Why did I do it? Why couldn't I have done things properly? Why did I take the office? I was too afraid, too proud. And now look at me. Olwyn was right to do what she did. It was an act of love. I was a fool, a hollow man, and found out big-time.' He pictured himself casting the alb over his head, knotting the cincture, moving beneath the heavy hood of chasuble and standing all glory, the loneliest man in the world.

Harvey came back to Crystal's place. Crystal was standing there, looking at the white mitre in Harvey's pink, trembling hands. Harvey began to tell him something.

'It's hard,' he mumbled. 'So hard.' But he choked up well and good, and lowering his face, bent the mitre between his hands. After a while Harvey looked up again. Crystal, like a faithful servant or altarboy, kept at his side. Harvey was breathing heavily, his mouth wide open, hands shaking more fiercely. 'It's hard. Damn hard. It hurt, it hurts. Oh God, it hurts so much I want to – ' But Harvey stopped there. Crystal looked out of the window, feeling in his crippled way for Harvey. But his face was blank, expressionless. His emotions were blunted.

'I'm cooking,' was all he said. 'Sausages and bacon.'

Harvey took a long time to recover, sitting like some victim of catalepsy, mouth open, eyes motionless, looking down at the floor. Finally, he came back to the land of the living, and put the mitre on top of the pile of second-hand clothes.

'I'm sorry,' he said weakly. 'I just feel so lonely.'

Only after standing over Harvey's bowed, silent head for a good while, did Crystal return to the kitchen and finish the cooking. Then, he and Harvey ate the burnt bacon, sliced the fat sausage, mopped up the oily juice with wads of bread. After the food was down they made themselves as comfortable as they could and watched the fire. Harvey prised his shoes off and let his toes steam. Crystal stepped out of his oilskins and sat on the sofa in his long-johns, a blanket over his head, and began a series of foul farts.

Crystal would have liked to have heard Harvey's story, with the fire so lively, and nothing to entertain him but his internal weather systems. But he did not press for the tale. When he lit up, Harvey couldn't help wondering if the air around him was going to combust. Crystal settled back into the sofa, playing with the smoke that left his mouth, blowing it downwards over Harvey's silver head. Now he blew it to the ceiling. Now slowly out of his cavernous nostrils.

Harvey just stared into the flames in the grate, the skin of his face reddening with the heat. He did not look round at Crystal, sitting in the cooler region of the sofa. Nor did he speak with him. Yet he was thinking about him: how Crystal had ended up in this cowboy hostel; about the hoard of tablets; the way he stopped people going where they wanted desperately to go; the voices; the paranoia. He marvelled at how he had come to share a room with this man. Was it simply from being destitute? Or was there some deeper sympathy? But Harvey grew tired of this line of thinking. He was here. That was it. Life was a roller coaster. And this is where it had taken him. It was determined. All he could do was try to enjoy the ride.

Roasting his toes, he began to wonder if he would be better off making a second visit to the jewellery quarter when it opened again on Monday. He might sell his watch. Then he might go to London. Although he felt uncomfortable with the idea of getting rid of the gift his mother had presented to him at his ordination, what else could he do? Sell the pectoral cross, perhaps. But Harvey still felt uncomfortable about exchanging that. He would only do that as a last resort. In the meantime, he would try to accept Crystal's strange but welcome hospitality.

7

The intruder light did not come on. Kilgarriff looked up at where it was bolted to the tree trunk, and made a mental note of getting Tourville to fix it, or have someone in to do the job. He felt relaxed this morning, and lazy, the dark sky cloudless, the air mild for the time of year. Unlike the day before, he had no wish to punish his body, drive it too hard. He decided to do an easy jog along Route Two. He pulled the zipper of his tracksuit up, drawing the fabric tightly around his chest. The last patch of gravel crunched under his feet. He turned left down the lane, away from the main road, lifting his knees as high as he could manage, shaking his fingers loose, getting rid of yesterday's lies.

As he passed behind the old stables, the roof just visible over the wall, he took a satisfied breath of air. He rolled his head a few times, stretched his jaw and jogged on, looking at the rich, wide house fronts of his neighbours. Nothing stirred. No lights sneaked into the morning darkness. Not one dog ran out to nip his heel. On his left, his own garden opened out, with its statues, greenery and swimming pool, dark beneath the horse chestnut.

He thought about what he had said to the parishioners in Hickley. Only white lies, he told himself, like feathers from a dove. There's no harm in them. Besides, how else could he run the archdiocese? Politics came into it; they always did. He had to think out all the angles, even if that brought lies tumbling forth from his mouth. The Little Sisters of Mercy had left the archdiocese years before. He knew that, but did his people? He doubted it. The Little Sisters could have rotted, and no one would have noticed. As it was they had grown old, with no fresh novices to take over their poverty. They had to be farmed out to various nursing homes. But they had served a purpose, if only as one of Kilgarriff's little lies. And he would throw down more lies if he had to. There was a stink rising on his patch, and he had to cover it. He would not let the Archdiocese of Southwick be ridiculed. That was not the game. He jogged on, eastwards.

When finally he finished his run, circling the hill, falling short of the wood and crossing his garden from the northern-most side, Kilgarriff was bright red and sweating profusely. He wiped his brow, sprinkled his fingers over the lawn, and entered the house at the side. As always, he went and showered before joining Tourville and Rose in the small private chapel for Mass. The wood-panelled chapel had a unique stained glass image of the Sacred Heart. Rose always sat under it, getting a kind of spiritual transfusion.

Tourville became altarboy again on these occasions, bringing over the chalice and water, cleansing Kilgarriff's blunt fingers, ringing a little brass bell as His Grace lifted the bread and wine, bringing more water to rinse away the blood that hadn't slipped down Kilgarriff's fat throat. Rose was the congregation, saying the responses, listening intently to the readings and Gospel. On this morning, Kilgarriff rushed Mass, and did not sit quietly as he did most mornings before giving the closing prayer. Instead, with the candles working on the darkness, he signed the cross in a flash and went out into the kitchen for breakfast.

Rose hung on, eyes on the Sacred Heart, while Tourville tidied up in the corner of her eye, drying the little silver cruets, straightening the altar cloth, placing the tasselled key beside the tabernacle. He came over when he finished and bent low over the pew and informed Rose that she need not come to work on Monday. Her need to be needed made her flush. Why didn't they need her? But she never asked. She knew the Cardinal was coming to discuss the sensitive business of Bishop Harvey. She nodded at Tourville and let her eyes fix on the glass Heart again. She would not gripe. She would profit by a free day. She had lots of chores to do at home. Besides, she was not built for complaint.

In East Vale, Harvey woke to a miserable, dirty light. Crystal still slept, huddled against the back of the sofa, sunk in the gap where pennies are lost. He was snoring heavily and looked as if he might sleep on for hours. The oilskin had slipped from his shoulder and his skin, so white and blotchy, looked underfed, pathetic, like lard. Harvey stood up, his black shirt falling down over the tops of his legs, and went to the window. He felt stiff and cold and filthy. Outside it was wet, the rain driven by a sharp wind that was busy nudging television aerials. Leafless tress got the same treatment. Yawning in stages, Harvey stretched, let go a shiver, and crunched his eyes tight at the wet, dismal scene. There was no comfort in it. Not a drop. It was a day for the unemployed, luckless and lonely. Reaching down, picking up his holdall, Harvey quietly left the room, careful not to stir Crystal. He made his way along the landing to the bathroom.

There he transformed himself. Inside the stale, cramped room, with its scum-line round the sink and tub, Harvey regained a sense that he still had a future; that with a smooth chin, marble teeth, combed hair, soaped armpits and normal clothes, things were not as bad as all that. True, he had to use toilet paper to towel himself dry, but the effect was encouraging. He hadn't lost his desire to keep himself clean. That was something. He looked with a glimmer of pride at his reflection in the mirror, wiping his palms up and down the blue jumper, running a finger under the neck and setting it straight.

He arranged his few toiletries in the holdall, careful not to contaminate the mitre, which he had hidden beneath a clean vest and pants. He returned to the room. One after the other, he rolled his grimy shirt and trousers into a ball and left them on the mattress. But then, realising he had left his money in the trouser pocket, he undid the bundle and took the last of his funds. The sound of loose change chilled him.

Crystal was still flat out on the sofa. Flat out with his mouth wide open and stinking. Harvey made no attempt to wake him. He was glad to be free of him and have time to think. And in his nearly new garments and cheap training shoes, he paced quietly around the room. The leather of the shoes was stiff. Harvey curled and stretched his toes to try to soften it.

Crystal did not wake till nearly eleven o'clock, and even then was not really awake till gone noon. Meanwhile, Harvey had walked down Pinckney Road, bought a newspaper, and sat on a bench outside the Queens Head reading it. His reading was only disturbed by the whirr of an orange tram taking a few worshippers to church, a few footballers to the park, and others to the huge hypermarket on the outskirts of town.

Now and again, Harvey's thoughts kept switching to all that had happened. He felt ashamed at what had taken place. The consequences of his actions were like the feathers of a pillow shaken from a window, never to be gathered up. He knew that had his mother been alive, she would have been devastated by it all. He wondered if he would ever see Olwyn again. It seemed unlikely. He even thought about taking a train down to Tenby. But in truth, he could see no way of them getting back together. There was too much shame involved.

Now Harvey stood at the window, waiting for Crystal to slip into his oilskins. On his walk, Harvey had noticed a little convenience store and suggested to Crystal that they shop for a few provisions. Nothing fancy, of course. He could not afford that. But some essentials to keep them going. The rain and wind had dried and now, in the still bright afternoon Harvey could only feel Crystal was all the more inappropriately dressed as he stuffed his wool-socked haddock feet into his gumboots and picked up the floppy hat.

'I'm ready,' he said, crushing the hat onto his ill-kept head.

As they left the room, Crystal muttered under his breath to what Harvey guessed were his voices.

'Yes, I know what day it is. Sunday. Don't tell me. Yes, I know they'll tear me apart if I don't – '

Harvey said nothing, following Crystal down the stairs, past the closed door of the elegant room. Out in the road, Crystal looked round warily, then delved into his oilskins and lit a long nub he had found the day before.

Although it was not cold, Crystal had suffered enough winters to know that he needed a good stock of firewood to get through. As they walked on towards the shining tramlines, he thought about making a trip up to Roney Hill. Even though the place had been demolished years ago, there was still plenty of old wood lying about. The last time Crystal looked for such pickings he had found part of a patient's medical file. He had read it. It was full of notes about a burnt-out schizophrenic. Was he a burnt-out schizophrenic? Burned out like firewood. Surely not. His illness still blossomed. The voices still raged and abused him with foul mouthing. Most likely they raged because he didn't take his medication. But the tablets had been turning him into a husk of a man.

Crystal's fear and suspiciousness were high. His strange need to waste other people's time still bubbled up inside. The Time Wasters forced him to carry on with the task or face the penalty. And he knew what that was. Christ, he knew what they had in store for him.

Sunday had always been distressing for Crystal. It was the day of rest, a day when he couldn't waste people's time very easily. After all, most people were only too happy to waste time on a Sunday. There was hardly anyone in a rush. Any victims he chose would be more likely to laugh and wink at others. They would not feel time whittled from them as they might on a Monday morning. They would hardly mind his bizarre surgery, his removal of seconds, minutes from their lives. Time assassins like him had a bad day of it on Sunday. Mondays were different. But it wasn't Monday, and Crystal's fear was rising and the voices growing more foul-mouthed.

'I know they've got to hurt. I know that much. Fucking bastards. Yes, it's Sunday. Don't I know it? Quiet as stones.'

And so he carried on, Harvey walking a little in front, crossing the tramlines, disturbed by what he heard, concerned at the downturn in Crystal's mental state. Yet Harvey himself did not feel threatened. He felt he had gained Crystal's trust. It was Crystal who was sweating and looking fearful. It upset Harvey to hear him struggle with the voices in his head. His eyes filled up, and the inevitable compassion he always felt for people like Crystal swelled in his heart. Although he felt low himself about ending up in this kind of company, there was something right about it. It was perfectly imperfect.

The convenience store was down from the Fighting Cock and just opposite the Queens Head. Outside the ramshackle building, with its strange concrete pelican looking down from the roof, Harvey rummaged through various boxes of vegetables and fruit. Most of the Christmas trees had been sold. That shocked Harvey. He had forgotten, or perhaps had chosen to forget, that such celebrations were fast approaching. He went inside and wove up and down the narrow aisles while Crystal waited outside.

When Harvey finally emerged, Crystal looked disappointed at the half-filled carrier bag. It fell like a starved breast from his hand. It proclaimed yet more light and unsatisfactory meals. Crystal suggested they go up to Roney Hill Asylum and take the opportunity of gathering some fuel for the fire. Harvey couldn't see why not. The suggestion was comforting in its way. At least, thought Harvey, Crystal can get on with real things. He was not totally in thrall to his voices.

They passed the Fighting Cock, with its rust-coloured tiles, and took the next right. This lane wound northwards to a huge brick wall, far too high for anyone to scale without a ladder of some sort. It was the wall of the old asylum. No longer needed to prevent escape, it stood redundant, a symbol of the old institutional days. Harvey looked up at its never-ending blur, the swish of Crystal's oilskins brushing together like someone begging for silence. Harvey wondered whether the wall had really been to keep people in or whether it had been built to keep people out.

Soon enough the wall opened up where a drive cut through into a huge space of grass and rubble. And there they were, standing on the fallen trousers of a building, only its distinguished front remaining, its windows breeze-blocked. There was the quality of a cemetery about the place. What was welcome, of course, were all the odd bits of wood lying about. Plenty of it sticking up at the motionless sky. Plenty enough for a winter's burn. Harvey watched as Crystal stooped and delved, lodging several large pieces under his arm. Harvey helped find more, putting his meagre shopping down, trying not to scuff his nearly new stonewashed jeans. Crystal returned with a good pile under each of his thick arms.

'See there,' Crystal said, using his head to point. 'That was my ward.'

Harvey nodded and felt pleased that Crystal wanted him to know a snippet of his history.

'Just there. See? That mound.'

'What was it like?'

'Okay if you did what they told you. I made a big mistake once and paid for it.'

'How come?'

'Well, a hospital inspector came and I was chosen to tell him what I thought of the place. I told him the food was very good indeed, and that we had a nice warm dormitory, and lovely grounds to walk in. And then I said that the staff were very helpful because if we did anything wrong they would set us on the right path with a damn good beating.'

'As bad as that?'

'Sometimes. But it was still, well, it was my home. It was better than the shit-hole I have to put up with now.'

Crystal bustled past, stumbling over the bricks, heaving the wood tight under both arms. He stopped on the overgrown lawn. He turned and smiled broadly. He dropped the two bundles of wood.

'I remember, years ago,' he said, 'there was this patient, Fred. He sat just here as if he had discovered grass for the first time. His hands were trembling and moving all over the place, touching, touching, touching the grass. I've never seen anyone look as happy as he did. His eyes were bursting with joy. And the next time I looked at him, he was standing up. His one hand held up his pants and the other was stuffing a frog into his mouth, its little legs kicking. I have never seen anyone look so happy since, champing away like this.'

Harvey laughed at Crystal's imitation of Fred.

Crystal picked up his sticks again, and they both said no more as they left the way they had come. But as they descended the hill, back towards East Vale, Crystal began answering the voices. He jerked his head at them. Once or twice he nearly lost his hat. Harvey kept his distance. He couldn't help but think that Roney Hill should be opened up again to protect people like Crystal. But which was worse, the institutional bullying or the cold community? He shook his head and thought again of Fred eating the frog, eyes staring, completely ecstatic, one hand holding up his pants.

While Harvey spent the rest of the day alone at the hostel,

ruminating in front of a generous fire, Crystal went out again, no doubt to see Molly at the station, or get up to his old tricks despite the quiet. He had gone with great urgency. Harvey had watched him from the window, scurrying along Pinckney Road, ignoring Mrs Angel with her terrible eyelid, who by chance crossed his path. Harvey felt uneasy about Crystal. He wondered how mad he was. Was he falling deeper into madness? Was he becoming a danger to the public, to himself even? Harvey contemplated all this.

Now he lay dreaming, dark fallen, his loose cheeks hot from the flame, his fingers zipped across his chest, holding onto a can of half-eaten corned beef. He had lost his appetite, and it had been all he could do to seek sleep, to settle the ashes of a dull afternoon. Pangs of guilt and loneliness mingled. He felt a complete failure without hope of redemption. Everything he had ever done looked so cheap and hypocritical. Fortunately, the heat of the fire helped him to drift and forget for a time his misery. And now, nothing disturbed him. On the edge of sleep the road kept silent. No one climbed the stairs to the bathroom. Mrs Angel had no visitors. Just Harvey's breath and snuffle and the burning, singing wood. In his sleep he returned to the island of Caldey, and onto the cliff path. There was Olwyn, and the lighthouse stark against a dense, black sky.

The predicted storm had come. And nothing – not even the rain that had built up over the previous days – could have prepared them for the deafening violence of the waves slapping the rock, and the lightning burning the air.

Harvey was wearing a black cape the Abbot had given him, which flapped wildly like tarpaulin. The wind was so strong that both he and Olwyn had to lean right into it to keep on their feet. And with his arm around Olwyn, he had to shout to make himself heard above the din. He asked her if she was enjoying the elements as much as him. He didn't need to ask.

Her green eyes were flashing with exhilaration. As the wind thickened, it filled Harvey's cape, and threatened to send him reeling over the edge of the cliff. If he had jumped into the air, this might easily have happened. But he bent low to the ground, and clasped tightly the two sides of his cape to prevent it filling like a sail. Olwyn's face was wet and reddened. Her little white fingers kept the collar of her red, glossy coat pinched at her neck. Spume like rising snow whirled upwards out of a cove and against the blackened sky.

'This is great!' she screamed, her coat moulding to her body. Her mouth opened only slightly as the rain stung her face. Harvey pulled her close as they walked awkwardly, perilously close to the edge. The wind buffeted them backwards into the deeper, wet grass. As if three-legged, the unlikely pair stepped through gaps in the dry walls, or gingerly went over low barbed wire. Where the fields inclined, Olwyn struggled on the oily grass and slipped. Harvey steadied her, holding her cold, wet hand firmly in his. The touch was electric. And they held hands longer than required.

At the top of a rise, they looked back towards the lighthouse and were surprised at just how far they had walked. At this end of the island the cliffs were higher and the waves did not thump over them in a white shroud. But the wind chopped fiercely and made Olwyn's hair chaotic. Harvey still had her hand in his, and while their fingers did not interlock, the pressure of the grip had strengthened. Harvey had a lump in his throat with this new level of intimacy. His belly ached just as it did when they sat together in the enclosure and he had so desperately wanted to kiss her. Yet the expected loosening had not yet come.

They continued walking, and now Olwyn seemed to be increasing her clasp of Harvey's hand. There was a glow between their palms despite the rough weather at their knuckles. Little by little, Harvey's mouth was opening wider to exhale. His neck was bumping with blood, and the beat of his heart was flabby. When Olwyn drew him closer still, his legs became wooden and foreign to the rest of him, his mouth almost permanently open to the rain, his air steaming backwards. Then Olwyn interlocked her fingers and sent Harvey's eyes out of focus. As he blinked and gulped, drowning in the years of dryness, Olwyn declared herself.

'I love you!' she shouted above the storm.

Now Harvey was in an emotional minefield, stepping one way then the other, altering his line, building a fearful sweat that was washed away by the rain and wind as it appeared. What should he do? How should he respond? He reflected on how much time they had spent with each other. Not just the swimming, or visiting the enclosure, but the nightly walks down to the beach to look at the lights of Tenby and talk.

They veered off, towards the cliff edge, into the wind. Harvey struggled to keep upright. Desire swelled inside him. The tin can he had kept base emotions locked up in for years felt dangerously pressurised, like a grenade.

'I love you!' Olwyn shouted again.

Harvey failed to respond. His loose hand was feverishly at his hair, stroking it down against his scalp, only for the wind to lift it free again. The storm was closing in. The gap between the flash and bang shortened. Olwyn stopped in her tracks and took Harvey's other hand, drawing him towards her.

'You're so sweet!' she cried. 'No, not sweet.' She looked upwards, struggling to express her feelings. 'Look,' she said, her voice raised above the sea-crash, 'at first I thought there was no chance, you know, you and me. But I have to say it, Harvey. It frightens me, and I don't know what it might mean, but I bloody well love you!' She bit the words, tightening her grip on his fingers. Harvey was spellbound.

They stood on a ledge, spume floating up and catching

against their bodies. There was nobody about. There was nobody to witness them standing close together, holding hands. Harvey let go and for a moment looked as if he had decided to turn his back on her. He seemed in agony. His face grimaced as he thought of all the times that he had been tempted before by flirting parishioners in their summer dresses. But he had resisted. He had denied the body. Now the ache in his stomach was of a different magnitude. It wasn't just lust. It was something altogether more powerful. His heart went out of beat, as it did when he drank too much, or ate spicy food. He felt bold and timorous all at once. As he stood apart from Olwyn, he was thinking of how well they had got on, their candid talk, her little touches of his arm or elbow. And while, in the tinder-dry monastery, insulated and alone, he had determined to return to his parish, out here in the wild, wet, natural scene, the idea of leaving Olwyn behind seemed perverse.

When he felt the urge to turn away, to remember his vows, and think of the possible hurt and confusion he might bring upon Olwyn by promising more than perhaps he could give, he thought about his own need to be loved. And didn't Olwyn deserve to be loved? If she was prepared to risk loving him, shouldn't he risk the same for her? Over and over, he battled for the grace to love. Just because I am a priest, he reminded himself, doesn't mean I can't have a loving relationship. Being celibate means I cannot marry. No more. No more than that. And it is just a rule made by men. Manmade, like the sole of a shoe.

Slowly at first, but then with determination, Harvey turned to face Olwyn and began twisting each large red button of her coat from its slit till it billowed open and flapped madly behind her. Olwyn steadied herself to the wind, half closing her eyelids, clenching and unclenching her fists as Harvey knelt before her. He placed his head close against her, sideways, dipped. For several minutes he kept this vigil, listening to the sea, absorbing the moment. He felt strong and free and no longer in crisis. The tin can inside of him burst open and thumped at his ribs. He reached up and unsnagged her thick skirt. It fell, ruckled around her boots. Olwyn's fingers grabbed at Harvey's silvery hair. Her wind-raw forehead lit by blue flashes, she urged him to his feet, slowly drawing his lips to hers. Her kisses became little bites, small desperate consumptions.

Towards midnight, Harvey woke up kicking out, his peace shattered, the corned beef can falling from where he had held it to his chest. In his dreamy state, he thought the roof had fallen in. There was terrible banging. The noise filled the room. He sprang to his feet, squinting in the dazzling light, trying to register what was going on. The huge figure that came smashing through the door and was now throwing its weight against it, hands flat against the walls on either side, resolved into Crystal. With his hands spread like this he leaned with all his bulk against the door. He had that hunted look on his face again. His lank hair fell down over his sweating nose, his blistered lip quivered, his oilskinned legs trembled as they pushed backwards, gumboots slipping and sliding, searching for a hold. He stared at Harvey, begging for help to keep whatever was pursuing him at bay. But Harvey just stood gormlessly in the middle of the room, his fingers glued to his cheeks.

'Help me,' blubbered Crystal, scared out of his wits. 'The Time Wasters are coming.'

Harvey frowned, shaking his head.

'The Time Wasters. They're coming for me. They're going to tear me apart!'

Harvey blinked life into his eyes. For a moment he thought Crystal was talking about real people, but then caught on. He went over to the window and looked out.

'There's nobody out there,' he told him.

Crystal laughed in desperation, tears on his lashes, froth at the corners of his mouth.

'They're hiding, for Christ's sake! They're not daft!'

Harvey felt a nervous smile tugging at his cheeks but resisted the muscular pressure. It wasn't that he saw the situation as funny. It was simply perplexing, and he did not know what to say for the best.

'Look, Crystal, you're safe now,' he said finally, approaching his crouched, pathetic form. Harvey held out open hands as he drew close and squatted down next to him. 'You'll be okay, I promise. Nobody's going to hurt you.'

Crystal shivered and kept pushing back against the door, sweat still dripping from him. Harvey felt his eyes well up. It was distressing to see Crystal so upset. He put a hand on his shoulder and squeezed gently.

'You're safe now,' he repeated in a low, nurturing voice. 'You're safe.'

'They can get to me still,' Crystal insisted.

'No,' reassured Harvey soothingly.

'Yes, they can. You don't know them. They told me what they'd do if I failed once too often.'

'No,' answered Harvey, holding Crystal's sobbing shoulder.

'It's not my fault. How the hell can I waste anybody's time on a Sunday?'

'Well, of course you can't,' agreed Harvey. 'They'll understand.'

'They, they force me,' he whined. 'They force me.' All this time the voices abused him and warned him to keep his mouth shut. 'I don't like doing it.'

The voices chastised him, and Crystal knew things were getting bad because they came from outside, not inside. He could cope with the voices when they were in his head. He could distract himself. But now they were on the outside, beating at his ears, and had power over him. Parasitic on his fear, they bloomed.

'I know, I know,' he heard Harvey break in.

Harvey swallowed hard as Crystal curled up into a ball. The sight pulled the tears from his eyes. Harvey had never cried so much in all his life as he had done over the last week. Not that he saw tears as something to be ashamed of. He never thought that. But it pointed to where his life had ended up. And when he looked upon Crystal's raw, suffering face, he could see a little of himself there. Like Crystal, he too was a reject. True, there was no real comparison. Harvey had the best deal. But still, he was sharing the same chill bathwater as Crystal. He had joined Crystal in a run-down hostel for ex-mental patients in a community that cared little. Harvey looked out through the window and saw that it was snowing in lumps.

8

Harvey dug his fingers into the soft mortar, gritting his teeth, and needling free yet another chunk from between the inter-locked bricks. It was hard work and the tips of his fingers stung. Now and again, he swung a sledgehammer at the wall, fearing the sound of it might alert people to his strange activity. He would have been happier if he could have got away without using it. But the huge hammer was the only thing that would loosen the bricks and, holding his breath, he would let it fly. Yet most of the work went on quietly, Harvey digging at the wall with a screwdriver and his fingers.

Another clump of plaster came free, dust floating down, his eyes watering as his fingernails scratched and dug their way deeper. He took a breath and saw the mess he had made of the cornflower bedspread, the ash carpet, his black trousers. Every-thing was covered in a pinkish brown dust, even the corners of his mouth. He wiped his hands dry, took up and plied the screwdriver almost noiselessly into the mortar-filled runnels. He felt driven. His throat bumped as he kept at it, as little by little one brick, then another, was freed and pulled from the wall.

Like a surgeon with gloveless fingers, he inserted the screw-driver, wiggled it from side to side, came out and went in again. Each time he took out a brick organ and placed it carefully to one side. When the mortar refused to yield, Harvey picked up the sledgehammer again and swung a single blow so as not to give a listening ear the time to home in on repeated strikes.

Gradually, the mortar softened with his persistent effort. ore and more lumps came away. This spurred him on, spite the dust clogging his throat. Hot and bothered, prickly at needling his scalp, blinking away the onslaught of falling st, he kept to his task of dismantling the wall.

Through the window, the sun flooded in, making him even ter and more irritable. While August had been warm, tember was sweltering. Down below, the parched and ow grass bounced the sun's rays into Harvey's tiny room 1 its wire-latticed bed that creaked each time he fell back t to rest.

e did so now, his fingers burning and his arms aching at elbows. The dust on the bedspread juddered as he sank it. Slowly the dust settled on his wet forearms as he lay : breathing wildly, his mouth wide for air. The screwdriver from his sweaty hand onto the floor, and he reached up jelly fingers to unbutton his black clerical shirt, trying to himself down. His tongue poked out, muddied slightly plaster, stringing what little juice remained between his ritty teeth. His blue eyes stared up at the hole beginning ear in the patchwork of brick. The ripped edges of the mbossed wallpaper dwindled away like strange tentacles. ing his gold watch in front of his face, Harvey realized must prepare for Confessions. Annoyed, he struggled bed and slipped into the bathroom to run the shower.

With his dirty clothes puddled on the cork mat, and with a fresh set of black on his body, he looked as priestly and innocent as ever. And only his fingertips shone guilty red. Only one other person knew what he had been up to that afternoon. It seemed unlikely that anyone on the street, or next door in the grounds of the church, would have heard the thudding sounds or scraping. Sounds which could resume after Confessions.

Harvey disliked Confessions, yet had incorporated them into

his life like so many church duties, and in truth, Saturday evenings would probably feel strange without them. And at St Patrick's, it wasn't so bad. In the little soundproofed room, with its slide-back grill through which fewer and fewer people confessed their sins, he could sit quite comfortably in the breeze of an electric fan. Now, slipping into his shiny black shoes, he licked his lips, anticipating the whipped, icy air on his warm face.

Some priests liked to hear people's confessions face to face. But not Harvey. It was bad enough knowing the voice behind each sin without seeing the sinner. And it was bad enough being a bishop hearing confessions. Somehow, he felt that those who slid back the grill for his ears expected a greater penance from him than they would from an ordinary priest. But he never satisfied them in this way. He sent them home, often as not, with the request that they do nothing more than sit quietly and reflect on who they were and what God wanted for them. He never thought himself worthy to hear the sins of others, and many times felt like asking a penitent to listen to him instead. To listen to all his dark side. To wipe his slate clean. It would be better, and truer, he felt, than going to a priest who didn't know him; one from outside the archdiocese.

Pulling the pectoral cross straight, Harvey went downstairs, along the hall and out into the vestibule. Before opening the front door, he checked his hair in the mirror for telltale dust. There was none, he was certain, even around the rim of each nostril. Yet did it matter? Need he be spotless? For Harvey had begun to believe in the imperfect. He was as seriously flawed as anyone else: a bundle of contradictions. Whatever he had done in his life, he always succeeded in falling between two camps. Always middling. Always almost, but not quite.

He drew back the solid oak door and stepped outside into the shade, waiting a moment, looking out over next door's overrun garden, the For Sale sign still flattening the long grass.

No sooner had Harvey left the presbytery than Magdalen appeared. She knew Harvey's clockwork habits and routines. And she always managed to be within shot of him whenever he emerged to do Confessions. She would alter her pace along the road so as to meet him on the driveway up to the church. And she would be there, too, kneeling like the few others in the confessional box, hoping that he recognised her voice, and that he might be drawn towards her raw, privately conducted sins.

She came now, so predictably, her long tasselled skirt hiding her legs, which never saw the sun and which she hated. But she liked the rest of her body, her long brown hair, big eyes and lashes. Now she crossed the road and judged her speed to perfection as Harvey stepped off his path. Sometimes she sensed Harvey played a game with her. He would stop at the end of the path and look as if he were about to return to the presbytery. This would catch her out at the last minute and make her feel awkward. It was an art to remain inconspicuous. It was an art she did not have. But he did not play today.

'Ah, good evening,' he said jauntily, opening the gate and pulling it closed behind him.

'Hello, My Lord,' she said, with a spring in her step, her tassels swishing at her sandals. She lifted a hand to draw a hair from her dry lips. She was about forty years old. But she never talked age. Birthdays were like little deaths. As always, she was fantasising about being his housekeeper.

'Hot enough for you?'

'Too hot,' she complained.

Harvey said no more. He knew Magdalen of old. He knew she liked to put her face to the words behind the grill. He knew that her confessions were really the sin itself.

She drew close to him as they turned to walk up to church. She smiled happily, thinking how wonderful it would be to look after him. For she knew his lot: how lonely he must be, struggling to keep clean shirts in his wardrobe, eating at irregular times. And she saw herself as being the ideal person to put all this right. One of these days, she thought, she would ask him directly if she could be his housekeeper. After all, it was not fair to leave him unsupported and isolated in his presbytery. It was her duty to pursue the matter.

Just then, Harvey's neighbour emerged from the newly sold house, slamming the door behind. Magdalen was first to look round, knowing only too well what she would be looking at, but she did not allow herself to be intimidated.

The house, which had stood empty and dilapidated for so long, had been bought by a single woman. And no ordinary woman at that, Magdalen saw, jealous that she herself did not live elbow to elbow, shoulder to shoulder with Harvey. She would have bought the house herself had she the means to do so. The woman was a professional of some sort, Magdalen guessed from her clothes. More than this, she had legs Magdalen only dreamt of. Long and elegant, glistening stockings, quite a sweep to the hemline of a pink dress suit. She turned from her front door, walnut hair swishing from a powdered face and gooseberry eyes. Ridiculous eyes as far as Magdalen was concerned: unreal and plastic-looking. She had no doubt that the woman wore contact lenses to give colour to dull, common irises. Besides, she was plain, and with this thought, Magdalen stared boldly at her, but not for long. This woman matched her look as she advanced down the path, not batting one eyelid, oozing confidence and strength where, in truth, there was little.

Magdalen withered under the gaze of the woman, and stopped staring.

'Hello,' Harvey greeted the woman. 'How are you settling in?'

'Sorry, do I know you?' she answered harshly with a lilt to her voice, difficult to pin down.

Magdalen gasped with shock. How dare the stranger greet a bishop in that way? She drew closer to Harvey, mouth open, and saw him flinch a little.

'I'm your next-door neighbour,' he told her, rubbing his smooth round chin. 'Bishop Harvey.'

'Bishop?'

Magdalen narrowed her eyes and gritted her teeth.

'Here?' she said, gesturing behind her. 'I thought bishops lived in mansions.'

'No, no. I prefer to be among the people.'

There was a glint of light in the gooseberry eyes. She frowned and let her straight, poppy lips bend downwards as if disapproving.

'So that monstrosity belongs to you,' the woman told him, looking towards the church. 'It almost put me off buying in this area.'

Magdalen rolled a fist at this. Treating Harvey with such disrespect was one thing, but having a go at the parish church was another. Yet she said nothing, expecting Harvey to reply in a robust fashion. But rather than putting the woman in her place and cutting her dead, as she willed him to do, Harvey answered in a tame manner indeed.

'It belongs to God,' he said.

'Does it really?' was all she said, rather sarcastically, staring hard at Magdalen, before turning on her chocolate stilettos and walking away in the opposite direction. Magdalen just watched the little stiff, leather butterflies glued to each heel and wanted to tread on them, crush them, beat them to the ground. But her anger was just too strong and she stood there, stomach clenched, churning up juices. For a long time her mouth stayed open, dumbstruck by the rude neighbour. In the end, Harvey took hold of Magdalen's elbow.

'Can you believe that?' she gasped, watching the receding figure of the woman. 'And she's living next door to you. Now

I thought the last lot to live in that house were a bit funny, but she takes the biscuit. The cheek!'

But Harvey said nothing, trying hard to conceal his amusement. He absorbed Magdalen's fury like a sponge, flirting a little with her, jolly and light-hearted. And she willingly took his compliments like bread on her tongue.

Molloy saw them approaching, and disapproved. He stood in the porch by the holy water font. He saw the way Magdalen held her face for Harvey. And he disliked the fact that Harvey did not seem cold to that look. He always thought priests had to be especially careful with the women of the parish. He took care himself, although he never suspected they would bother with him. But Molloy kept on his guard for any kind of intimacy, especially touching, even from men. He felt that too much touching softened the will. That is why he squirmed and pulled away when Harvey threw an arm over his shoulder as a greeting.

'Well, I'll go into my box like a horse again.'

After listening to a few confessions, with few blots of sin worth the listening, Harvey set off back to the presbytery with Magdalen in tow and Molloy left behind to close up the church. Like a detached shadow Magdalen moved down the drive alongside the bishop. She had spoken her transgressions so clearly, without distorting her voice, as she did as a child, and let her secrets melt through the grid like hot butter. She looked into his face now and again, reading him, knowing that he had her secrets as chemicals in his brain. Let me be your keeper, she willed. I would be good to you. I would be so good.

They parted with a wiggle of fingers, but when Harvey closed the presbytery door behind him he grimaced as if he had chewed a lemon. He went straight upstairs, lifting off his chain of gold and quickly unbuttoning his black shirt. He hung the chain over the post at the top of the stairwell and changed back into the dirty clothes he had thrown on the bathroom floor. Then he went into the back bedroom and got to work. The heat was oppressive and he made slow progress on the wall, digging fruitlessly at times, struggling to wheedle yet another piece of mortar free. Eventually, with sweat curling down his back and from under his armpits, the wall began to loosen. Again and again, he forced the screwdriver in, rocked it from side to side, sometimes hitting at it with the ball of his hand to drive it deeper. Once or twice he wielded the sledgehammer.

After some time, and with the day fading, Harvey had loosened the mortar sufficiently to bring several bricks free with his fingertips, stacking them with the others on the floor. He prised and bullied them out. He was through to the next layer now. Again he took up the screwdriver, wrapping his blistered palms round its handle, and dug wildly, too tired to be fussy, each stroke tugging at his raw flesh. But clamping his teeth, with his shirt clinging to his spine, he was determined to finish the job before sundown. He soldiered on, his muscles weak, his face stung by chips of flying brick. And as he did so, he hoped no one could hear out on the street. No one must know what he was doing.

Not far away, Molloy was busy in the sacristy. He had heard the occasional dull thudding sounds, but dismissed them. Hickley was full of do-it-yourself fanatics. There was little else to do in a town like Hickley. From where he stood, he saw the presbytery, its garden fence, the tops of the apple and cherry trees. And everything was as it should be. Nothing was happening. He bent down and pulled out a shallow drawer full of candles: milky white, shiny like the skin of the dead. Molloy ran his finger up and down them. All these candles had been used, but considered worth using again. He took a knife and trimmed them, cutting away melted wax until each blackened snuff could hold a flame. Frowning as he worked with the candle close to his chest, bits of wax tumbled down his black cassock and onto the worn rug.

Back at the presbytery, Harvey was making progress. Now the wall had a peephole, and he looked through it into the house next door. It was the bedroom. Breathing heavily, licking his dusty lip, he saw candy-pink wallpaper and a small heap of clothes piled up on a bed. On the wall hung an oval, cloudy mirror, in which he could just make out the hole which he was staring through, as seen from the other side. This excited him. For a while, he felt like a peeping Tom. He remained with his face pressed close to the wall, spying the emptiness of the other room. But then, out of sight, came a noise which slapped his heart into action, making it pound irregularly at the root of his neck. She was there. She was back, waiting, tantalising. Through the dust, he picked up spicy perfume. His nostrils widened to take it in. He felt light-headed.

Eagerly now, he pushed his face right up against the hole and sniffed, closing his eyes, teeth slightly apart, forehead tight on the chipped plaster. For quite some time he stood like this, silent, intoxicated, breathing heavily. Then, small bumping sounds broke open his eyes, and chocolate stilettos fell into the middle of the bare floorboards, as if each of the butterflies at their heels had suddenly tired of flying and fell to the ground. He said nothing. His lungs juddered. Then, a stocking zipped downwards through the air like the softest arrow, crumbling at its fall. Then another, making him ache for sight of the woman he loved. A pink jacket followed, then a skirt, both spinning down to the brown, stained wood. Harvey whispered her name now. But she did not speak. The fall of an ivory blouse kissed his eye with its wind, and dropped out of view. Then white frilly knickers shot across the oval mirror and hung like a tiny parachute from the table lamp.

And there was Olwyn, standing with her back to the far

wall, her feet slightly apart, holding her breasts together, closing them over the scar that had lost her so many men. Her green eyes seemed to fade and glow in the sheltered light from the table lamp as she moved towards it and then turned it off.

With the darkness flooding his eye, Harvey returned to the digging, picking up the screwdriver and poking madly at the thin veil of brick that blocked his passage to Olwyn. His muscles were pumped up and fierce. The stinging blisters were forgotten. Twisting and jamming the screwdriver into the mortar, he worked without a break. He was hungry now. He took his bare hands to the job, ripping and yanking with all his strength, even clawing and punching the wall. One by one, the bricks came away, the hole widened, and soon looked large enough for Harvey to squeeze through.

Harvey wasted no time poking his silvery head through. Then came his arms, his chest, until he was able to scramble upside down into the darkness on the other side, brushing a space in the debris for his palms to take his weight. If the mirror could see him, he would have looked absurd, hanging down, a strange foetus. The dark was softening now, a little light filtering through the window into the room. He could make out Olwyn standing by the bed. She came towards him, a creamy blur. Edges were broken down and lost. Harvey lay on the floor, breathing noisily, bits of brick pressing into his body. Olwyn brushed spaces in the debris with her feet. And slowly, while Harvey squinted up at her, she crouched down, her long, thin fingers wrapping over her knees, her moist flesh catching motes of unlit dust like an exotic flower catching flies. Slowly, she spread out and engulfed him.

'Oh God,' he moaned, wrapping her close, a hand cupping her head and drawing it down into the crook of his neck.

'I've missed you,' she whispered, arching back, her eyes catching the poor light from the window.

'We've done it,' he said. 'And no one knows.'

Harvey ran his fingers back and forth across her ribs, pulling her into him, occasionally ruffling her hair, so glad to be near her, smell her. He shifted on the rubble that dug into his hip. It was painful. But it was good. It was different.

'What an idea,' he whispered, staggering the words, a little burst of air from his nose. 'No one will know what we're doing. Now Magdalen will tell everyone how rude you were to me. They will never suspect you of being anything but a neighbour from hell. They will see what we want them to see. You live in your house. I live in mine.'

He sighed, satisfied with their plan, and raised his hip again in a lively fashion. It had been a long three months sorting everything out, and now Olwyn was in his arms again. He felt the weight of her. He felt the trickle of her breath on his face. He thought of the day she was waiting for him on the steps of Tenby Harbour. It all seemed such a long time ago: all their secret meetings and walks on Caldey, the passionate embrace in the storm, lying down in the tall grass beyond the farm, or behind the white lighthouse, or in the prehistoric cave over-looking nothing but the sea.

'We will not be seen as anything but reluctant neighbours,' said Olwyn. 'Nothing but neighbours that don't get on. No more seedy hotels or bed and breakfasts. Now I'll be able to see more of you.' She kissed him on the temple, and then each comma of dimple.

'Time together. No more portable love. We shall move as we please through this wall.'

And he remembered all the different one-night rooms that they had stayed in. Always in out-of-the-way spots away from Tenby, away from Hickley. Not that he regretted those meetings. How could he? His skin now felt his own. It had made contact with more than bathwater, clothes or bedsheets. Olwyn had touched him into wholeness, or so he felt.

'Love you, Ol,' he said.

'Love you too,' she answered.

For ten months, since they met on Caldey, the secret meetings had been going on. And ten months of change had taken place. Not only had Harvey adapted to a love affair, but he had quickly adapted to the responsibility of being a bishop; not any bishop, but England's youngest. No sooner had he returned from his retreat on Caldey than he learned the news of his preferment. He felt favoured, successful, confident. And he felt more complete; like the time before his mother died. He sensed he belonged to the world and had a purpose. He felt justified in taking Olwyn as a lover because she gave him the strength to serve the people. She kept his head tilted above the water to draw the air he needed. But being with Olwyn complicated matters enormously. There was no doubt about that. However, since Olwyn was not pressuring him to marry her, he felt he could remain in the ministry without compromising his vows beyond chastity. He knew of other priests who had done the same. To his mind, Olwyn was the fullest expression of grace he had ever received. And now Harvey was determined to go on seeing her without anyone finding out.

Now they could live side by side without suspicion. It was Harvey who had the idea of buying the house next door for Olwyn to live in. Of course, he did not have the money to do this, but Olwyn did, and she pursued the purchase. More than this, she saw the possibilities for living even closer to him when she recollected a weather house she had seen as a child. From one door of a colourful model of a house, appeared the tiny figure of a woman whenever the weather turned fair. From another door, a man appeared whenever the weather deteriorated. It struck her simply: two doors, one house.

The previous owner set a reasonable price for the house, and Olwyn did not hesitate in giving the asking price. She was determined to have Harvey within reach and sensed that perhaps, in time, she might get him to leave the ministry and

125

commit himself fully to her. But she knew that would not happen overnight, and kept hidden her desire to walk hand in hand with him in public. She wanted the normal experience of introducing him as her boyfriend, and even husband. But for now, she held back her rumbling desperation for a more permanent relationship. And Harvey, still with lust clouds in his eyes, failed to see the dangers in crossing the road of love.

Harvey could not step out of his cassock that easily. He had been a priest for fifteen years. He had grown used to the clerical life, and impressed everyone with his natural intelligence and caring nature. Giving up something he had invested so much time and energy in would be difficult. In essence, Harvey was not best suited to wake up to the real world. In many ways, his ministry had sent him to sleep. To wake up now would be a shock. It would be asking too much. Especially now that he had been made a bishop. He preferred, instead, to continue his relationship with Olwyn in a naïve fashion, believing that, somehow, the Church and Olwyn could remain separate like oil and water.

And here she was, lying, sweating beside him, tracing a finger over indentations that the rubble had made in his back. Through the gap in the curtains, only darkness. Olwyn smiled deeply with satisfaction, marvelling at the act they put on for Magdalen. That the world should see her leave by one door, and he another, while within they could move like bees through the hole. Perhaps it should be bigger, she thought. Harvey could extend it into a proper doorway. But it was enough for now that they had access to one another. This side of the summer, she was happy. This side of the summer, she could bear the privacy of their love. Olwyn's mother knew nothing of the affair. She was used to Olwyn's business trips and visits to craft fairs up and down the country, and had not questioned her prolonged absence. If anything, she kept her fingers crossed that her daughter's travels might bring her into contact with eligible men. To that end, she gladly ran the craftshop single-handed.

Sore from lying in the rubble, Olwyn and Harvey got up and took a bath together. Harvey took the plug end, and lying back in the hot water, they marvelled at what they had achieved. Originally, they had considered only making a gap in the garden fence and visiting each other that way under the cover of darkness. But the hole in the wall was better. It guaranteed invisibility from the many prying eyes in the dull town of Hickley. The hole in the wall eased any fears that Harvey and Olwyn entertained about being discovered. As far as people were concerned, all was as it should be at the presbytery of St Patrick's. Everything was above board.

When the presbytery telephone rang, it sounded distant and redundant, and emphasised Harvey's removal from his duties. Yet, lying in the bath with Olwyn, he ignored the nagging sound. Whoever it was could wait, he decided without too much guilt. He just carried on washing Olwyn's dusty hair, spilling water from his cupped hands over her stooped head. When he had done this, he lathered the yellow soap into her flesh and rinsed the suds with playful splashes that made Olwyn squeal with delight. In a gesture of acceptance, he removed her hand which covered the scar on her chest and kissed the ugly mark. At first, she pushed him away, but Harvey insisted and returned his lips again and again, giving little pecks all along its route between her breasts.

'Thank you,' she whispered, giving in, tears standing on the edge of her eyes. 'Thank you so much. That means an awful lot.'

They embraced and sat motionless in the water. Little wavelets were sent out by their booming hearts. Olwyn's wet hair clung to Harvey's shoulder and drops of water tracked down their curved, naked backs. All was quiet. Away from the world, from prying eyes, these two incompatibles held onto one another, moistly joined, Olwyn's fingers digging into her lover's flesh, Harvey's lips moving back and forth on her shoulder as if he were playing the harmonica. Here were the bishop and the scarlet woman. But there was no glamorous or exotic sin here. It was human, common, fumbling. Both had been victims of loneliness. Both had struggled for a sense of completion and belonging. Was it such a crime to do what they were doing? Of course, they knew it wasn't ideal. It wasn't how to go about things in a perfect world. But where was the perfect world anyway? The dark, frosted window above them rattled an answer.

After bathing, they dressed and went downstairs. Olwyn entered the front room first, drawing the newly hung curtains tight, making sure there were no gaps before turning a lamp on. Only then did Harvey feel safe enough to sit down on the large, blue leather sofa. He could smell its newness and fiddled with the manufacturer's tag that Olwyn had not yet removed. He examined the stinging blisters in the crook of his thumb and palm where the handle of the screwdriver had dug. There were no blisters on his left hand; just a few scratches where the brick had caught his skin. His black trousers and shirt were very dusty and, despite the bath, Harvey still felt dirty. In fact, this was nothing new for Harvey. He had always felt dirty.

'I'll have to make the hole larger,' he said, fingering the blisters, looking up at Olwyn who now wore a large tee shirt and fluffy blue slippers. Combing out her hair in the mirror that stood on the mantelpiece, waiting to be fixed to the wall, she looked at him and saw him inspecting his hands.

'Are they hurting?'

'Yes, a bit,' he said. 'Mostly where the screwdriver caught me.' He opened his hand, which had become red and angry-looking, and was unnerved by the mark which looked like a nail had been driven through the flesh.

Olwyn pulled her wet hair into a tail and tied it with elastic.

'Ah,' she sighed, crossing the room and kneeling in front of him. 'Let me kiss it better.'

Harvey sucked a whistle as her lips touched his raw palm.

'Gosh, that looks sore.'

Harvey said nothing. He was wondering what explanation he would give people for the damaged skin. He thought that he might put it down to a spot of gardening.

'Shall I make a tea?' she asked, patting his knees and getting to her feet. 'And I think I've got some antiseptic cream somewhere.'

Outside, unnoticed, Magdalen slowly passed by on the other side of the road, moving beneath the umbrella of street light. She looked enviously at Olwyn's house with its bright blue curtains, a vague shadowy light upstairs bleeding through nets. Then she looked at the presbytery, all dark, uninhabited. But she had Harvey tucked up in bed, saying his *Nunc Dimittis* or fiddling with rosary beads. And she wished she could be with him, her head next to his, his breath warm against her cheek. Little did she know that she was addressing her dream to a cold, empty bed, crisp and unruffled, no dent in its pillow.

'There,' said Olwyn, putting the tea down on the floor and then twisting the cap off a tube of antiseptic cream. A worm of white squirted onto her finger, and she applied it to Harvey's palm. He smiled happily with the attention.

'Just like a married couple,' she chirped, her finger circling his stretched palm. Her words were not lost on Harvey, but he chose to ignore them. He did not want to think about what she might be desiring, deep down, and what eventually might bubble up to the surface. He knew there would be a price to pay further down the line. But for now, things were fine. For now, he would try to keep reality from breaking in. He just wanted to be with her. That was enough. How permanent the affair would be was something he did not have the appetite to consider. Olwyn continued to nurse his hand, knowing that it was a breakthrough to get this far, to share intimacy and closeness with the man she loved and not have to crawl in and out of hotel rooms anymore.

Olwyn knew Harvey was devoted to the Church, and should he leave, all his years of ministering might seem worthless. After such a time, she guessed, Harvey resembled a limpet clinging to its rock, for fear of the freedom of the sea. He had told her how his vocation began as a child, turning his wardrobe into a little chapel where he spent hours praying with a candle burning dangerously close to the wood. He told her of the loneliness that came with taking his vows, and of being different. She could smell this on him. She didn't need to be told. And he spoke of his mother who, Olwyn suspected, had been an obsessive Catholic.

Olwyn's mother wasn't like that. She had lapsed from the church and preferred to call herself a freelance Christian. For some reason, she had left the fold. It was something she did not wish to speak about and which lodged in her throat like a fishbone. On the matter of religion, Olwyn chose to float, ignoring her baptismal tag.

'I'm so happy,' she announced, working another blob of cream into Harvey's palm, convinced that she would be the one to prise the limpet from its rock. 'Okay, I know I have to put up with a private love. I know that, but to have you here, in my house. To know that we can move through the wall, out of sight, behind closed doors. It is enough.'

'And the deception? What about that? Do you mind it?'

'Why should I?' she said. 'Even straight lines bend eventually.' And she knew how deception was a part of her life, of any life. She had accepted long ago that she was inventing herself daily, changing and defining herself from moment to moment. The idea was not so disturbing. She had worn down any teeth it had and made it a familiar thought. Like anyone else, she was a chain of trial-pieces.

'When it rains,' she said, leaning forward and kissing Harvey's grey head, 'you can leave your house; and when it shines, I'll leave mine.'

9

The weeks went by, and still Magdalen saw the enemy living next to Bishop Harvey, and cursed. Was it too much to hope that the woman left? Was it too much to ask that she re-erect the For Sale sign that now lay half hidden in her front garden? And there the enemy stood, in a short, provocative black skirt and lime top. Olwyn was looking down at Magdalen in a superior, arch manner, taunting her, it seemed. How Magdalen hated these chance meetings with no quality of a meeting about them. During these silent and almost daily confrontations, she wanted to poke out Olwyn's plastic-looking eyes, rip her hair, scrape her shins. All summer she had put up with seeing Olwyn's shaven, perfect legs, whilst keeping her own out of sight.

At least Bishop Harvey did not pay the woman attention. That meant a lot to Magdalen. In fact, that was her only delight. That two people could live side by side and not make small talk at the gatepost, or lift hands in recognition in the street, was unusual in Hickley. The people of Hickley were friendly as a kind of cover to know everyone else's business. If Harvey had shown affection to his sour neighbour in any way, however small, Magdalen would have been deeply hurt. But he hadn't as far as she could see. Not a jot.

She passed on, hoping that before long, Harvey's unworthy neighbour would get the message and leave the area. Magdalen knew she wouldn't, of course, but liked to entertain the idea.

Certainly, the woman was no Catholic. Magdalen was sure of that. If she was, she could only be one of the terrible lapsed. Anyone could see that. Without looking back, Magdalen crossed over, her tassels dragging leaves that had fallen into the gutter with her as she walked.

Olwyn shook her head, smiled and went inside. Silly little woman, she thought as she closed the door behind her. But despite showing such a cold front, and feeling the chill blast in return, Olwyn would have liked someone to talk to. Not Magdalen, but someone. Since moving in, it had been a lonely few weeks in many ways. Much of the time, Harvey was out visiting parishes, confirming the youth of the diocese with a slap across the cheek, or conducting any one of his many duties that seemed to grow and grow under the direction of the Archbishop. Even now, he was out taking more orders at Burnt Green. True, when they did see each other, sparks flew. There was passion then, and lots of it. But something deeper was lacking in their private love. On autumn's tail, Olwyn was doubtful about her future with Harvey. She thought she was mad to strike up such a relationship. At times, she sensed it was laughable. Now and again, she felt her desperation for his love, and despised herself. Yet being close to Harvey, even in a patchy kind of way, made her want more. She couldn't help thinking about marriage. The idea filled her mind and resulted in frustration. It wasn't too much to ask, she reflected. They had been together nearly a year now, after all.

She went upstairs with a heavy heart, pulling on the banister, sighing, doubting that her fingernails would ever get under Harvey's limpet nature, prise him from the rock, and fall back with him into the sea.

The back bedroom had been swept clean now. The hole in the wall was much bigger, almost resembling a doorway, but not quite high enough to keep her from ducking her head as she wandered through to the other side. Why did Harvey have to be a priest, a bishop even? Why couldn't he have been free like the next man? He could have been a coxswain or fisherman in Tenby, for instance. But no, a God man. How she wished to see him uncomplicated, at ease with himself, returning from the harbour, smelling of fish, instead of walking around with a collar round his neck. By now they might have been fixing up a nursery and doing the normal things.

To be average, boring, held a certain attraction. More and more she pictured Harvey digging the garden, painting a house front pastel pink or blue, or taking their children down to the beach. He would be Olwyn's husband. Olwyn, the girl with the scar down her chest, would have a husband. Olwyn on the shelf would be brought down and belong. Yet all that was uncertain in her crazy life with the bishop.

She lay down on the bed, hands behind her head, and attempted to figure things out. It wasn't the first time she had seen the folly of her circumstances. And it wasn't the despair that was the problem, but the hope. The hope that Harvey would step out of the cassock that was trapping him and do his duty by her. But would he? Could he? Wasn't there too much of the little boy about him? The eternal, naïve boy? Yet she loved him still. As her mind whirred, she chose to suffer the belief that somehow, bit by bit, she might change him. The limpet might fall back in her arms yet.

Out at Burnt Green, Harvey was following Kilgarriff down the path to the swimming pool, which sparkled in the sunlight. Only a section of the pool lay in the shadow of the horse chestnut tree. They both wore trunks: Harvey's a deep claret, Kilgarriff's emerald green. And as they walked, the sun dazzled against their pale skin. Kilgarriff was first into the pool, making a huge splash. Harvey diving and taking an age to surface, followed him. As Kilgarriff swam to the side, his dyed black hair plastered to his forehead, he talked in a lightweight way about the weather, the water temperature and the frogs that jumped in the grass. Then he began a frantic crawl down the pool and back again. Harvey admired the Archbishop's stroke.

'Race you,' Kilgarriff challenged after a few more lengths, keen to show how his body had maintained its strength despite the years of gravity.

'I'm really not very good,' Harvey tried to excuse himself.

'Come on, man,' coaxed Kilgarriff, his thick jaw sinking beneath the water, till just his brown eyes looked at Harvey. Then he spurted water from his lips, and shook his hair like a dog.

Harvey agreed reluctantly to the challenge, and was soon floundering in the middle of the pool, his breaststroke no match for Kilgarriff, who delighted in slicing his way to victory. As Harvey struggled back to the side, Kilgarriff laughed warmly and lifted an apologetic hand. But it was more of a salute. Like an old, dying superman, he bobbed up and down. Age hasn't touched me, he seemed to be saying. Fit as a fiddle. Fit as a fiddle.

'Well,' said Harvey, 'you're too good for me.'

'Ah,' he celebrated. 'Barry always says the same. Too much for me, he complains. Well, it just goes to show, if one looks after one's body . . .'

He kicked off again and did a slower couple of lengths, finishing off underwater.

When he came up for air, it was with these words: 'So how is it at St Patrick's?'

He lay his forearms on the poolside and squinted across at his newly appointed bishop.

'They treating you well?'

'Yes, I would say so,' answered Harvey.

'Good,' he said. 'I think we chose the right man, don't you?'

Harvey didn't know how to answer.

'I'm happy,' he told him, sinking into the water, drawing a little of it between his fine teeth and squirting it out again.

'And I'm happy,' confirmed Kilgarriff. 'You are more than qualified for the office. Your pastoral work has always been admired, you know that. And you have a fine brain. We couldn't have a better man on the job, as they say. But,' and here Kilgarriff stretched out his legs and began paddling to distract the sharpness of the question, 'is there anything you'd like to tell me? Anything at all?'

For a terrible moment, Harvey buckled, suspecting that the Archbishop had found out about Olwyn.

'How do you mean?' he managed to ask.

Kilgarriff kept him dangling.

'Oh, nothing in particular,' he said, making light. He knew nothing of Olwyn. But he knew how to dig. He knew that by pretending he had a spade, he might get Harvey to dig a hole for himself and reveal things that would otherwise remain hidden. It must all out, he would maintain. It must all out. Especially, when he had new men on his team. However much people were vetted for promotion, Kilgarriff liked to keep a watching brief, sweep up afterwards just in case.

'You have no worries with the job?'

'No,' said Harvey, trying to look at ease, leaning back into the water and floating. He glanced at the palms of his hands, glad the blisters had healed so well.

A silence followed, in which Kilgarriff left Harvey to his digging. But Harvey did not use the spade. He sensed the danger of responding to his own guilt and growing defensive on account of it. And Kilgarriff, not seeing a hole, turned back to the mundane.

'What about St Philomena's? Has that been sorted?'

Harvey floated upright.

'I've asked Father Winterton at Stonehill to carry the bleep. He has Canon Powers with him, so he shouldn't have too much difficulty getting off the parish. And he seemed quite keen about it. He's done chaplaincy before, of course.'

'Good, good,' nodded Kilgarriff. 'Ah, here comes Rose with the barley water.' She moved lightly over the grass, head cocked to one side, her bony fingers clutching the tray to her flat chest, the ice chinking against the crystal jug.

'I've put lots of ice in,' she said. 'It should be lovely and cold.'

'Thank you, Rose, that's great.'

She bent down from the hip, straight-backed, straight-legged, resting the tray on the side of the pool.

'Do you need anything else?' she asked shyly, joining her hands in front of her.

'No, Rose, that's just fine,' smiled Kilgarriff.

'Sure? I don't mind.'

'Sure.'

'Okay then,' she said, hardly creasing the grass, wisp of flesh that she was.

'So,' said Kilgarriff, pouring the barley water, and handing a glass to Harvey, 'here's to the youngest bishop in all of England.'

But as Kilgarriff raised his glass, Harvey was thinking about his illicit affair with Olwyn. For a terrible moment, he sensed that he was not just compromising the Archbishop, the Church even, but God Himself. He swallowed heavily. I need her, he reasoned. The loneliness is too much for any man. And until they allow married clergy, it has to be like this. After all, they've accepted married Anglicans as priests. Surely what I am doing is what so many others are having to do. At this point, he pictured what little remained of Southwick's clergy, all in white, at his consecration. If they only knew, he thought, what sort of bishop I am. Then again, it might do them some good. It might liberate them. All those, out there, lonely in presbyteries. The third sex. The deformed sex. But while Harvey admitted to himself his imperfect nature, he did not wish to have it broadcast to all and sundry. And certainly not to Kilgarriff. 'It must all out,' was not *his* battle-cry.

10

The day after Harvey's visit to Burnt Green, Olwyn was moody and sullen, and over the following week she was given to a brooding silence which built up on occasions into uncontrollable tears. Harvey did not anticipate such changing moods, and struggled to cope. At first, he thought she was ill, and then with a shiver of horror passing over him, considered that she might be pregnant. But she was neither of these. Besides, he knew Olwyn always took the tablets she kept by her bedside. He never mentioned the tablets, of course. He had spent years keeping off the subject of contraception, and he had no appetite to discuss such matters with Olwyn. She religiously took the little pills, and that was all that mattered. He preferred to close his eyes and hope they did what they were made to do. He took other precautions as well, so did not worry that Olwyn might trap him one day. He did not suspect such trickery. Yet the way she felt lately, Olwyn had thought of exactly that. She had entertained the idea of pregnancy as the only way of getting him to leave the ministry.

Try as he might, Harvey could not fathom what was wrong with Olwyn. Now she sat, half undressed on the toilet seat, crying, while Harvey perched on the bath, head down, fed up, frustrated. To his mind, there was nothing he could do or say to help. The roll of toilet paper which had fallen from her trembling hands lay at his feet. In the belief that he had caused her present misery, Harvey fell to making endless apologies.

For what, he did not know. He could not see his continuous crime. He just could not see.

'I'm sorry,' he told her, reluctant at first to shed a tear, feeling distant and cold, but then letting one or two dribble away from the corners of his eyes.

'Tell me what's wrong,' he pressed her. 'I can't bear to see you like this. Whatever I've done, I'm sorry. I'm sure I must have done something. It's me isn't it? Tell me what I've done to bring this cloud over you.' But Olwyn burst into another wave of tears, dipping her head between her knees, hair falling, almost brushing the floor.

'Sorry,' Harvey struck up again, getting off the bath and placing an arm round her shoulder. But slowly, in a stupor, she pushed his hand away.

'What have I done?' he insisted, upset at her rejection. 'Just what am I supposed to have done?'

'Just leave me alone,' she grunted, picking at her hair with what little energy remained in her. It was as if she were profoundly depressed. Perhaps she was. She wanted to say that their relationship just wasn't working; that it all felt wrong or out of kilter; that it was different to what she expected. How long could their temporary tryst go on? At first, it had seemed the right thing to move next door, to have secret access to her lover, but the doubts were setting in like arrows falling from a great height.

Sometimes she felt imprisoned or cornered. Where had her freedom gone? The weather house was losing its enchantment. What at first was novel and magical had become dull, predictable. It was ridiculous. What could grow from such secrecy, such hidden love, except disappointment? She was not getting any younger, and all the time, nagging in the back of her skull, was the shelf, the dreaded shelf. The shelf that made her feel more and more desperate.

Lost about what to do, Harvey rubbed his chin, turned

slowly, and left Olwyn in yet more waves of torment. Her sobbing could still be heard after he had stepped though the hole in the wall and returned to the presbytery. As he went downstairs, he feared someone might hear her if they visited him. But he had few visitors out here in Hickley. And at the bottom of the stairs, Olwyn's noise had been stripped away.

Harvey moved through the dining room and sat at the table, turning a napkin ring in his shaky fingers. As he fiddled with it in an aimless fashion, it dawned on him that Olwyn wanted more from him than he could possibly give. He feared that her dreams of marriage were sharpening. Just when he thought she had resigned herself to love behind the doors of the weather house, it seemed as if she wanted much more. The hairs stood up on the back of his neck. He wondered if she might do something silly; declare her love for him to the world. But he chased such thoughts from his mind. I'll pay her more attention, he resolved. When was the last time I bought her flowers? That will bring her back. But despite such thinking, Harvey couldn't help feeling that he was shuffling his feet closer to a bottomless pit.

Just then the doorbell rang.

He listened to it ring a second time, hesitating, and only after wiping his sweaty palms down his trousers and pausing at the bottom of the stairs to consider if Olwyn might still be heard, did he open the door. At first, he thought it might be Magdalen and dreaded opening the door to her. But drying his lips with one hand, he opened the door with the other, and peered out onto the doorstep.

'Hello, Father,' came the light, shy voice of an elderly parishioner, her knobbly hands purple-blue even in the heat of the day. She said no more, but hung on the doorstep, hoping to be invited inside. Harvey did not want to ask her in, but from the expression on her face felt he had no choice.

'Come in, come in,' he said, delayed, shaking his head quickly to get the blood circulating through it.

'Thank you Father.'

He showed her down the hallway to the front room, and she sat on the edge of the thick sofa, too nervous to lean back into it. Hunched up, she began to speak but lost her words, and gave instead a wrinkled, twitching face full of pain and unspeakable suffering. Harvey sat beside her, clasping his hands to his lap, opening his ears, receptive. She glanced up at him, but her eyes fell away like water droplets from a hot plate.

'What's the matter, Doris?' Harvey enquired, looking warmly into her twitching face. Wringing her hands, she finally spoke.

'It's Bill,' she told him. 'He's dead.'

Harvey's mouth opened at the news, then he frowned as he searched for an image of Bill. There he was now, selling the Catholic papers in the church porch, cap to the side, little ginger moustache in the filtrum of his lip. Bill, dead.

'When?'

'This morning, Father.'

'I see,' he said, gripping her hand.

'There was a crash bang, and when I ran in he was lying there slumped over the bath. I tried to move him, Father, but couldn't. He's still there,' she sobbed.

'Have you notified anyone?'

'No.'

'The doctor?'

'No. He's dead. A doctor's no good.'

Harvey tucked his arm around the slight figure of Doris and put his head close to hers, squeezing her hand. She shook all the more with his comfort. It gave her release, and what was bottled up came out. Only when she settled again and took out a handkerchief, chiding herself for being so silly, did Harvey break free.

'Come on,' he said, 'I'll help you sort things.'

'Oh, will you?' she said.

'Of course. You come with me, Doris.'

'I felt terrible leaving him like that.'

'You couldn't move him,' Harvey reassured her.

'But it's so undignified. He wouldn't have wanted to go out with his pyjamas at his ankles. Oh, Father,' she cried, 'it's cruel. I told him not to strain so much on the toilet – I'm sure it caused a stroke or something.'

Harvey stood over her, silent, feeling her pain. He had lost count of all the deaths he had attended. All different; all unique exits from the stage. Not one the same.

'You didn't call an ambulance, then?'

'I know the look of death,' she told him. 'I didn't want to add to things with sirens. I didn't want the neighbours a-looking and a-whispering.'

So Harvey left with her, and spent the whole day making the necessary arrangements, listening to her stories, making pots of tea, bringing hope where he could. He laid out Bill's body with the help of the local doctor, who said it was an expected death. Then Harvey gave the Last Rites, arranged the undertakers and prayed with Doris at the bedside. Towards evening, one or two neighbours paid their respects, followed by a few of Bill's relatives. Only when other people were there to keep Doris company did Harvey leave. Slipping out quietly, he returned to the presbytery dog-tired and uneasy about everything.

11

In and out from their different doors, Harvey and Olwyn moved through autumn, sometimes madly in love, sometimes not. Now the For Sale sign board lay covered with golden leaves, and the air which had been kind, grew cooler. Magdalen still told her hot secrets every Saturday, and gained nothing but relentless absolution; still she teetered on the edge of asking Harvey if she could be his housekeeper. Harvey went to his endless meetings, often with his umbrella tucked under his arm, or occasionally unfurled, shepherding nothing but rain. And despite his good intentions, he had never got round to bringing Olwyn flowers. Only now and again did they fall to the floor naked, or onto the sofa; but when this happened it was with desperation, as if in a panic to hold their love together.

The deep belongingness that Olwyn desired had evaporated. Harvey showed less and less affection. He hardly ever kissed, never mind licked, the scar on her chest. The idea of a public love had been swept under the carpet, and Olwyn caught the doldrums of shopping, cleaning and ironing, where her spirit dwindled. Often lost to the television or a stream of useless magazines, she considered returning to Tenby, her mother and her business. Even book-keeping had begun to look attractive.

'Here's the paper,' she said listlessly one morning, her gooseberry eyes dull from yet another restless night. Another night of rolling thoughts, of turning east and west for an answer. Harvey did not look up at her. But he listened to her padding across the kitchen floor, opening cupboards and starting breakfast. Then, he stretched back his head, unfolded the newspaper and began to work his way down the columns. Most of the time now, Harvey had his meals in Olwyn's house while his own kitchen took on an odourless, clinical appearance, with the bread tin gaping and kettle long dry. If Magdalen had seen his kitchen she would have despaired that it lacked a woman's touch and filled a bowl with fresh fruit, stocked the fridge, polished her face into the kettle, and made it homely. Such a drift to Olwyn's house was also reflected in Harvey's bedroom, which had remained untouched for weeks now, and in his dirty clothes, which churned in her washing machine.

Harvey lifted his eyes briefly to look at the drizzling rain coating the overgrown back garden.

'Beans or tomatoes?' Olwyn called.

'Sorry?'

She repeated the call.

'Beans,' he said finally, and thinking about the generally poor communication between them, added a thank you. But it only came out as a whisper.

Eventually, Olwyn placed a cooked breakfast in front of him, while he kept his face behind the paper. His face was still hidden in the news when she delivered the tea, milk and sugar. This time, she hadn't put the usual effort into presentation. Spilt milk was left unmopped. After a while, he folded the paper to leave an article of interest on show, and tucked into the food.

'Rioting again in Liverpool,' he mumbled, pulling a clean napkin from the silver ring.

Olwyn did not answer. Neither did she eat with him. She stood by the sink with a bowl of cornflakes, looking out through the misty kitchen window.

Harvey held for a reply, but when he didn't get one, shrugged and turned his attention back to the black print. But soon after, Olwyn did speak, although in a detached and distant way, just a disembodied voice from the kitchen.

'I don't think I can stand this for much longer,' she said.

Harvey looked up this time and listened.

'Holed up like this, diving for cover if the doorbell rings, feeling like a hunted animal all the time. I'm getting a cage mentality, you know, moping around, sitting and staring. Where's the life in that? It's downhill, Harvey, isn't it? Let's face it. It seemed like a good idea at the start. But I've become that strange beast: the priest's housekeeper. Now that's not for me. I'm a businesswoman, for God's sake! Love on the edge seemed exciting, but not now. Not now, Harvey. A house-keeper? It's worse than that! I don't get to answer the door of the presbytery. I don't get to give those enigmatic smiles that keep the parishioners guessing!'

Now Harvey winced, fidgeting with the sugar bowl, spooning granules and letting them fall.

'And it's getting colder in this weather house that we've built. It's as if we're beginning to fall for what others see – that we don't get on, that we live separate lives, that we have nothing at all to do with each other.'

'That's just not true,' complained Harvey. 'Now you know that's not true.'

'Oh, but it is, Harvey. It is.'

He got up and went into the kitchen. Olwyn was still standing by the sink, a vacant look in her eyes, an empty dish loose in her fingers, dripping. He put his arms around her, and kissed the back of her head. She did not resist. Nor did she accept. She stood quite alone in company, as if what was wrapped around her was nothing more than a cloak or blanket. And the more Harvey felt emotionally blocked, the tighter he

146

squeezed. And the tighter he squeezed, the more Olwyn fell into herself.

'You know I love you,' he pleaded. 'You know that.'

Olwyn let the bowl slip out of her grasp into the sink.

'You know how much you mean to me.'

Olwyn felt chill and remained silent, leaving Harvey no alternative but to produce a monologue.

'But I can't just give all this up, just like that. I can't up and leave, run off and marry you. This is how it must be, Olwyn. You know, behind closed doors. How else? And I hate it too, Ol. I would like to show you off. I would, honest. But it's not to be. We have to face that. I'm a priest. I'm a bishop. I know you're tired, sweetheart. I know that. And I know I haven't paid you enough attention with all the parish and stuff. But I'll make it up to you, I promise.' His garnet ring brushed fondly against her dry lips.

Harvey did not feel encouraged by her silence, but risked fumbling his way inside her dressing gown. She did not reject him. But, in truth, she did not really feel his fingers. She was just a whirl of thoughts, flicking up memories like leaves. Her body was numb, distant, dead.

'We'll go out tomorrow afternoon,' he whispered into her ear, his hands busy. 'Tomorrow afternoon, I promise. Just me and thee. We'll get away from Hickley. Go for a walk.'

And that is what they did. Travelling separately out of Hickley Station, they made their way to the Malvern Hills. The sky was clear and there was a cutting wind. Olwyn wore her red coat, with a green scarf, knitted by her mother, wrapped twice round her neck. On her head she wore a black beret, tilted backwards. Harvey wore his heavy, black overcoat, but no hat or scarf. They walked slightly apart from each other, in a meditative, ruminative way, as if building up to say something momentous. But nothing was said. And no one disturbed their silence. Usually, there would be someone out walking their dog, stick in hand, or hikers. But nobody passed by. Harvey promoted their isolation by keeping to the least popular tracks. The Midlands stood brushed clean and visible for many miles.

Olwyn had only ever seen the Malverns from the motorway, at a distance, grey and looming, rising from the flat. Harvey watched her taking in the view. He smiled, glad that he had brought her away from Hickley. Her company felt fresh again, and he moved closer to her. Olwyn eventually held onto the crook of his arm, which he pushed towards her like a folded wing. Her thoughts were elsewhere, however. Her head declined as she watched the lift and fall of her boots.

As they walked together, Harvey convinced himself that all was not lost in their relationship. He felt his appetite for her company returning. And feeling this, he grew determined to plug the gaps and fill in the doubts about their future together. He resolved to speak the things she wanted to hear and move closer to her way of seeing the world. He resolved not to take her for granted.

'What do you think?'

'It's lovely,' she said, lifting her head quickly and looking about.

'Yes, it is quite lovely,' he echoed. 'If you look out there you can see Burnt Green.'

Not that Olwyn wanted to see Burnt Green.

'There,' he said, pointing beyond the ridge of Hickley Beacon.

'We've not come far, then?'

'Far enough,' answered Harvey. 'Far enough to relax together. Just you and me.'

Harvey thought he caught a smile building in Olwyn's face.

'I know I haven't been very – well, I've been a fool. I've let things slip and I'm sorry. You see, Ol, I'm still learning. I know I've been lazy with the housework and all that. And I don't just want you as my housekeeper, Olwyn. I'll try harder.'

Olwyn squeezed his arm, encouraged a little by what he said, and Harvey picked up the change in her mood, and lightened his talk on the back of it.

'It's a bit like the cliffs on Caldey up here,' he mused. 'All that land could just as well be the sea.'

Olwyn nodded, thinking about Caldey, and their time together on the island, and began to wonder if she and Harvey could work something out after all. Perhaps, in time, if she were patient, she could find a way of turning him into a normal husband; no longer defined by his dead mother; no longer bound to his ministry. In time, she might remove him altogether from the rock he clung to. Then she thought about her desperate need for love. She had felt the ice-burn of loneliness for too long now to wish it back.

Beneath his coat, Harvey wore his clerical shirt minus the collar. Even the shirt was camouflaged in a burgundy cardigan. Despite being far away from his parish, he dreaded meeting someone he knew. He caught himself raising a gloved hand to his face or rubbing the brow of his dipped head when people approached, shielding his jowls from eyes as much as the chopping wind.

Olwyn sensed how uncomfortable he was but said nothing. She was thinking now about her own mother. She hadn't contacted or visited her for some weeks now, and made a mental note to ring her that night. It was always good to hear her voice down the line, to picture her standing in the living room above the shop, harbour at her back, framed in the large window. If only she knew what her daughter was up to.

Harvey and Olwyn climbed the hills. He felt happier now. The silence between them had been broken and things aired. That afternoon, Harvey had hoped for simple togetherness, a lungful of fresh air, and the spirituality of grass, leaves and sky. And that is just what he achieved. And by the early evening, they walked down from the hill to catch the train back to Hickley feeling optimistic again. They sat together on the train until they approached the beacon, when they separated, and in the long tunnel running through the hillside to the town beyond, they looked complete strangers, sitting back to back. As the train came to a halt, they alighted from different doors, walked to opposite ends of the platform, and took exits that divorced them further.

At first, the trip to the Malverns seemed to do the trick. Olwyn and Harvey got on much better. Throughout September, Harvey kept his promise and gave her more attention. He cancelled trivial meetings and spent quiet evenings with her, curled up in front of the television. He even bought her flowers. Unfortunately for Harvey, Magdalen caught him walking down the street with them, and looked decidedly puzzled. After all, she was the flower lady. She was the lady who kept the vases of St Patrick's full of colour. And it would have been no trouble for her to make up a bunch for the presbytery. But when she complained, Harvey praised her flower arranging skills so highly that she instantly forgave him.

Olwyn appreciated the show of affection and lost some of her doubts and fears. She even began to break her general isolation by chatting with people in Hickley Town, becoming known to the shopkeepers, and joining in with idle chit-chat about the weather and suchlike. As she opened up a little, she felt and looked less of an outsider. She did the normal, routine things. Now and then, her presence was acknowledged with a wave from one or two of her neighbours. Never Magdalen, of course.

But any optimism Olwyn had in September was wiped out in October – a wet, miserable month. Nothing happened in that chapter of time to keep a votive candle of hope alive. Harvey filled his life with church business again. He hardly spent any time with her. All he gave her were the titbits of an evening, or the last folding-up hour before bedtime. Through-out the month, Harvey visited all the nooks and crannies of the Archdiocese of Southwick. At one point he spent the whole weekend in Westminster, discussing ecumenical issues with Cardinal McNutt and the Apostolic Pro-Nuncio.

Thus, by November, Olwyn had had enough. Though she gave Harvey several warnings that she wanted to see much more of him, nothing changed. Harvey began to sink under the labour of being a bishop. In turn she lost composure and grew increasingly depressed, taking to her room and crying endlessly, it seemed. Bit by awful bit, she could see all too clearly that her desire to have him for herself was going to be thwarted. She lost heart in the task of wheedling him from the rock he clung to. If anything, Harvey had grown more faithful to his various meetings and appointments. He rarely showed her the affection she needed. More and more, his kiss slipped from her mouth to her cheek, grew lighter, less intense, till it was nothing but the brush of a moth's wing to her. This hurt her deeply. And it hurt her to see the natural, loving, exciting side of Harvey drowning in church business. He was looking old again. The grey hair was beginning to suit his ways. His big, old, serious head was on. His blue eyes looked hard. It was as if, beneath the roof of his mitre, his thinking had changed, his warmer self erased. He was, she could detect, becoming more and more the bishop, and less and less her lover.

And so it came, that in late November, Olwyn walked through the weather house for the last time. It was not an easy decision for her to reach. She had desired to make Harvey whole, normal, natural. She had wanted to fall permanently from the shelf into his arms. But he was resisting. He was rooting into the church. The sense of his responsibilities as the shepherd to his people had returned with passion. Time after time, he had ignored her desire for him to leave the ministry and do right by her and convert their private love into something proper. But it was not to be.

Stopping briefly at the hole in the wall, she ran her hand down its dusty, ragged edge and mulled over what she had decided to do. He would hate her for it. But it was the right thing to do in the circumstances. If she could not have him, the least she could do was save him from living a lie. Before going downstairs, she pushed the small wardrobe in front of the hole, hiding it from view.

Harvey was at St Patrick's saying Mass, totally unaware that Olwyn had packed her bags. These stood in the hallway now, ready for when the taxi arrived. Olwyn would instruct an estate agent to nail up a For Sale sign and sell her house. A quick sale, she hoped. If it was quick, they might not move the wardrobe and see the gaping hole in the bedroom. Although she saw how impulsive she had been in buying the house, Olwyn would not lose out financially. The properties in the area had boomed since Hickley had been earmarked for inclusion on a high-speed rail link to London.

Now her sad poppy lips turned inwards, and her wet eyelashes drew together into little black spikes. How lonely she felt. How ultimately lonely after a fruitless year with Harvey. Perhaps she should have omitted the pills after all and driven him out of the Church with a baby on his back. But she could not stoop that low. It was no way, she decided, to bring a baby into the world. Yet even with a child to bargain with, she wondered if Harvey would have done anything more than what so many priests and bishops have done over the years: kept the fact hidden.

Listless, she moved through her side of the weather house, everything looking stark, hopeless and jaded. The oval mirror froze her black jacket and skirt, neatly combed-back hair and disappointed eyes. Again, her poppy lips twisted with pain and regret. Her leaving had come. It had been inevitable. And she felt strangely resigned to it, exhausted by the tug of love. While the shelf loomed, the mad tug of love had hardly made her happy.

But leaving, and doing what she was going to do, lay heavily upon her. She knew that she had failed to rip the limpet from its rock, but thought it was within her power to force the rock to reject the limpet. An act of love, as she saw it. She did not imagine her actions would benefit her, but she could not simply leave Harvey as he was. She would try, she decided, to set him free.

With this thought, she descended the stairs and waited in the hallway, perched on the largest suitcase till the taxi bibbed its horn. When it finally did, she left the house quickly, fearing that Harvey might return and spoil everything. She beckoned to the driver to help her, which he did, though reluctantly, flicking his cigarette high into the air.

Then she walked down the path for the last time, the For Sale sign still in the grass, the blue sky falsely optimistic, the air chill. Briefly, she looked back at the two houses, pressed together like praying hands, and shook her head. Then, without further delay, she crept into the taxi and it sped off.

'Where to, lady?' asked the driver, lighting up another fag.

Olwyn looked at St Patrick's disappearing from the back window, the outstretched arms of Jesus somehow imploring her to stay, or just lost for words.

'Burnt Green,' she said, and pushed herself back into the seat.

Magdalen had watched with glee as Olwyn got into the taxi, bags and all. She skipped off the pavement into the gutter and stared at the tiny black cab pulling further and further away. The legs she so hated were leaving Hickley. And she guessed, though she wasn't sure, that her enemy might be leaving for good. Her exit looked more permanent than merely taking a holiday. And these thoughts were confirmed within minutes when a plain white van drew up outside and a man nailed a bright new For Sale sign to the gatepost.

With joy in her heart, Magdalen crossed over and made her way to St Patrick's. In five minutes, Harvey would finish saying Mass. And she would be first to give him the good news. More than this, she thought with a burst of confidence, her tassels lively against her rushing feet, I will be his housekeeper.

12

Monday was the best day for time-wasting. The rush to work, London-bound trains heading out of Templeford Junction. The trams full to the brim, hanging on a sparking thread. All the hustle and bustle. A day precious to Crystal. A day when the voices did not abuse him if he looked sharp and did what they told him. It was a day when the Time Wasters kept their distance, let him get on with it, and did not scare him out of his wits. Unless it was Bank Holiday Monday, that is. But it wasn't. This was a normal busy Monday. And Crystal was up early to get his victims. First, on the tram into town, he found a man looking at his watch too often. Crystal sat beside him and pretended to fall asleep, and when the man stood up to move into the aisle, Crystal blocked him. He made him miss his stop. Then, on High Street, he just stopped people willy-nilly and talked garbage, slowing them right down. When finally they escaped his glue, they had to hurry along on the slippery snow. But it was at Templeford Station that the best pickings were to be had.

Back in East Vale, Harvey woke long after Crystal had left. And he woke to a bitter, clinging cold which set him shivering and made his teeth chatter. He squinted up at the icy window. Beyond the glass, a murk of falling snow made poor light. Whatever else, he was far too cold to lie back on the damp mattress. In a rush, he jumped up and quickly dressed, hopping into his jeans, pulling the buttoned, stale shirt over his head, tucking every bit of warmth in before putting on his jumper. Then he lit a fire. The paper he used was damp and it took a good while before it caught, Harvey blowing candyfloss to get it going. He was glad when flames wobbled upwards. He held out his palms and warmed them.

He remained at the fire, poking at the wood, his eyelids, cheeks and brow hot, until hunger pangs bothered him, and he knew that with such cold, only food would properly heat his body. Yet, looking out of the window at the snow-covered bag of provisions, he did not feel like doing his own cooking. Besides, the window frame looked jammed solid with ice. Instead, he decided to go into Templeford. He had enough money left over to eat at the café in the square, and anyway he knew he had to visit the jewellery quarter a second time, a final time, to sell his watch.

On his way into town, his black overcoat wrapped tightly around him, he had flashbacks from the night before: of Crystal's panic; his fear of things unseen. And he wondered about his plan of taking what money he might get for his watch and heading down to London. Christmas was coming, and sharing it with Crystal was not something he relished. True, Crystal had given him shelter which he desperately needed, and he had lent him his blankets and mattress. Crystal did not reject him or harp on about him being a disgraced bishop. Yet the idea of Christmas with Montgomery grew in Harvey's mind. Knowing him, it would be lively. Knowing him, it would keep his spirits up. And wasn't the fear of not locating him, of being homeless in London, no worse than the fear of spending Christmas in East Vale? Certainly, Harvey had begun to feel uneasy in Crystal's company. Crystal was in decline and unpredictable. What he might do scared Harvey. And even though Harvey had never been attacked by a mental patient in his life, he knew that there was always that possibility. It was a thought that jangled his nerves.

Harvey didn't take a tram into town. He preferred to walk in the snow, despite only wearing training shoes. He looked incongruous in his formal black coat, jeans and trainers, but no more than many of the people he met on the road. Besides, the walk helped to clarify his mind. In particular, he struggled to reconcile heading south and leaving Crystal to his own devices in the hostel. He could imagine the kind of Christmas he would have. He saw the landlady with the terrible flickering eyelid laughing and drinking with friends in her pretty room, while upstairs Crystal lay on the sofa, just smoking, alone, tormented by voices. But Harvey battled to be realistic, to whittle his compassion. After all, Crystal had spent numerous Christmases without company. He didn't need Harvey. Harvey couldn't cure him or make him happy. Perhaps he would leave him some money and just go.

Templeford looked deserted. Only a few brave shoppers trudged the pavements. The trams, complete with little snow-ploughs, stood empty at the terminus. Harvey guessed Crystal would be at the station with Molly, and hoped to pass through the town without bumping into him. He walked quickly, head down, slipping occasionally on the snow. Over the bridge he went, past the black taxis and on down into the square. Snow-free patches lay beneath the market traders' awnings, and here and there a few people clubbed together, blowing heat into their hands. Harvey did not look at them. Neither did he look at the pigeons tucked up on the ledges of buildings. Still the snow fell, in lumps, melting on his coat, making it infinitesimally heavier.

When he got to Greasy Joe's, he was more than ready for a hot tea and something to eat. He went in and was soon served an egg and bacon sandwich, something he hadn't had in years. The egg yolk dripped onto his plate. Harvey didn't mind making a mess with his eating. He was ravenous. The corned beef he had eaten the day before had merely glazed his stomach. He took a seat near the draughty door. It was an unpopular spot, but Harvey was grateful for the isolation. He didn't want to sit near anyone and feel that pull for conversation. He champed through the sandwich, making his chin yellow with yolk, wiping it with the back of his hand. As he ate he closed his eyes and nodded rhythmically, as he was prone to do when enjoying his food. Soon enough, he wolfed down the lot and brushed crumbs into the large crack that ran down the middle of the dirty table. The mug of tea that the girl brought over to him didn't last long either. Harvey had no wish to hang about more than he had to. If he was going to cut ties with Crystal and head off to London, then the sooner he got on with things the better, and that meant going down to the jewellery quarter and rustling up some more funds.

Harvey left Greasy Joe's and crossed the square in the direction of the jewellery shops. He was unsteady on his feet, keeping his hands outstretched like a rope-walker to balance on the snow. As he went he wondered how much he would get for his watch. It was such a beautiful piece of workmanship. In fact, quite unknown to him, his mother had spent a small fortune on it. Harvey inspected its dull green, mottled face and the gold fingers. It must be worth more than the ring, he guessed correctly. The more he got for it, the better chance he had of having a more comfortable few weeks. After the watch, of course, he could always sell the cross and chain. That would surely prevent him from living in the gutter or having to crawl back to Kilgarriff, tail between his legs. Determined to get a good deal for the watch, he saw what he intuitively thought might be the best shop, Wiggetts & Sons, even though it sounded like a funeral directors.

Wiggetts & Sons had thick blue carpet and a fan-heater just inside the door, which blew all the chill off Harvey, ruffling his hair as he stepped inside. Thankfully, the shop had no other customers, since trade was slow. He smiled at the young, smartly dressed man behind the counter, hesitating a little. But the young man appeared easygoing and friendly, telling Harvey just to ask if he needed help. Harvey slipped his watch from his wrist almost immediately and approached the assistant, who stood tall over the glinting glass display unit.

Harvey's dimples came out in a nervousness all of their own.

'I'd like to sell this,' he told him, hoping his mother would forgive him.

'Let me see.'

Harvey slid the watch towards him and then rubbed the pink mark where the piece had been secured to his wrist.

'Nice,' said the man. 'Very nice. Uninscribed.'

He turned it over and over in the palm of his left hand. He had the expression of a much older man.

'How much did you want for it?'

'I know it's valuable. But I'll be quite honest, I haven't a clue how much I should be asking for it.'

'Yes, well, it's a bit out of our range. As watches go, this is pretty rare. You don't see many about. Was it a present?'

'Hmm,' answered Harvey painfully, scrunching up his face.

The young man whistled, making a closer inspection.

'How does five hundred sound?'

Harvey didn't answer.

'It's worth more than that,' the man admitted, 'but it's shifting the thing, you know.' He placed the watch back on the counter and looked into Harvey's eyes.

Harvey's mouth had opened wide gradually.

'As much as that?' he answered finally.

The man nodded and smiled warmly.

Harvey put his hands over his mouth and nose and stared for some moments at the timepiece. His spine tingled with gratitude for his mother. Little did she know that he would need the watch to dig his way out of a crisis. But five hundred pounds was a lot of money at this time. It would help enormously. It was a fortune in his situation, rolling across the land, a virtual pauper. He wiped a tear from his eye, looked at the young man and decided that here was a man quite unlike the butcher who knows how much fat he can leave on the meat.

'Five hundred is fine,' he mumbled to himself, still in a state of disbelief.

The youngest of Wiggetts' two sons counted out the cash into Harvey's palm and took the watch, thanking him for bringing it in. 'We'll find a good home for it,' he said cheerfully, but sensing that perhaps this was not the best phrase in the world, sucked the air as if he had just received a needle prick. 'Sorry,' he said under his breath. Harvey never heard him.

Harvey left Wiggetts & Sons into blizzard conditions and had to draw the collar of his coat right up to his ears. It entered his mind to go straight to the railway station and board a train for London. But he had left his holdall at the hostel. Besides, he felt less in a rush now that he had a small financial cushion to fall back on. Anyway, it would be extremely rude and ungrateful not to thank Crystal for his hospitality and perhaps give him some money to help him along. After all, Crystal had kept him from the gutter these last few days, and the least Harvey could do was show his gratitude. He guessed Crystal would still be at the station, getting on with his strange, unfathomable business of wasting people's time. He would leave him be, let him get on with it.

On his way back to East Vale, Harvey bought an *Evening Post* and scanned it to see if they had printed any more rubbish about him, but there was nothing. Happy that the mustard seed had yet to grow into the biggest of trees, he cast the paper aside. He just wanted to be forgotten, left alone to merely exist. Since Friday he had not been followed. Or if he had, he hadn't noticed or been concerned to check. As far as he knew, there was no one on his trail, and even if there was, what could they learn? But he guessed that there was someone out there digging up the dirt. But for the time being, he didn't let it worry him.

This day had been a particularly good one. He didn't want to wallow anymore. Now that he had sufficient funds to move a little more freely, at least for a few weeks or so, maybe a whole month, he gained a spring to his step. I'm surfacing, he told himself, as he walked to East Vale. He thought about where he had been, the deeds he had done, and who he now was. I'm surfacing, he convinced himself. I'm coming up for air.

13

Rose had taken the day off without a murmur of protest. Not a critical word passed her lips. That was something she just wasn't built for. Tourville had stepped in rather keenly with rubber gloves and apron, cleaning the house from top to toe. Howard & Johnson, the caterers, arrived in good time and put on a good spread. Tourville dealt with them. He didn't want any waiters this time, he told them. The mob would feed themselves. He had been down in the cellar earlier in the day, choosing wine. He had brought up several bottles of Chianti and some particularly fine Barolo. Quite rightly, Kilgarriff had insisted on Italian wine since McNutt was an old boy of the English College in Rome.

'Not the Brunello,' Kilgarriff had warned Tourville. Not that McNutt disliked the taste, but he had told Kilgarriff long ago how he drank Brunello when he first met the Pope and wanted to preserve that singular, high point by not drinking it again.

Now Tourville sat with Kilgarriff. Everything was ready. Everything stood prepared. Looking out into the snow-covered garden, down at the iced-over pool, they waited for McNutt and the others to arrive.

'I wonder where Harvey is?' mused Tourville, stroking fluff from his black trousers. 'I wonder what he's been getting up to? Do you think he's all right?'

Kilgarriff grunted, took out one of his long cigarettes and lit up.

'Do I look as if I care, Barry?'

'It's very cold. I wouldn't fancy being out in it, you know, homeless.'

'No, I'm sure you wouldn't,' growled Kilgarriff. 'But Harvey has proved himself a resourceful fellow, hasn't he, Barry?'

'Even so, it is freezing.'

'You are beginning to sound like one of those awful weathermen. Yes, it's bloody cold, Barry. Well observed. But who took their ring and pectoral cross with them? Things that don't rightly belong to him. And don't think for a minute he hasn't got some money somewhere. Even if he is, as you put it, homeless, which I very much doubt, he'll roll back this way, believe me, with a tear in his eye and a whimper. Sometimes I'm sickened by our own generosity. He enjoyed *bodily* comforts too much, Barry. Mark my words, he'll come crawling back.'

Across the snow-laden grass, Kilgarriff's footprints from his early morning run along Route Three broke the pure, crisp, unspoilt blanket of white. But new snow had covered each bootprint. The heavily burdened horse chestnut gathered more and more of the sticky flakes of drifting snow. The sky looked clogged with it. Kilgarriff took a brooding drag of his cigarette, pinched his eyes together and contemplated with bitterness the shame Harvey had brought upon him personally and indeed Mother Church. But he felt happy that the newspapers had nothing more to say. For now the disbanded, non-existent Little Sisters of Mercy did their work well.

Kilgarriff flicked his eyes at the silver-plated dishes, lace doilies and pyramids of food. Tourville, who sat quietly on the other side of the lamp stand, by the table, breathed into his pale, cupped hand, testing the quality of his air. He didn't smell the onions that were usually there on a chain from his foul stomach. He dropped his hand and licked his lips. He was hungry and willed McNutt and the lesser lights to hurry up.

But he knew the thick, wildly blown snow must be hampering them.

When they did finally arrive, they came in dribs and drabs, as if to punish Tourville's acidic, expectant stomach. Among the first to bridge the weather was Canon Gregory, who had wisely come over the hill towards Burnt Green, sliding downhill from the north. Others rose miserably from Burnt Green, having to leave their cars at various stages on the hill. One of these was McNutt.

McNutt was grateful to bring his blue nose and snow-plastered white hair inside. Folds of ancient skin hung at his neck like the spoils of wisdom. He was desperate to be holy. Youthful eyes darted this way and that as Tourville took his coat and brought him through into the main lounge area. The hand he gave Kilgarriff was as papery as ever. It was the hand he had offered in all kinds of ways in the prison camp in Java. Now his hands were mottled and lean. Then they were strong like his head, which had suffered many beatings for the sake of the weaker prisoners. Surprisingly, perhaps, McNutt loved the Japanese. He held nothing against them, even though in the tide of war they had killed his dear friend Billy. All that was left of Billy now was the battered black-and-white photograph that McNutt had found in the slimy mud by his wrecked body. Billy was eighteen when they flew a bullet through his brain, a brain McNutt had loved deeply. 'I bloody loved that dear boy,' he would admit.

'How are we?' Kilgarriff asked him.

'The heart's daily battle with death continues,' McNutt chuckled cheerfully. He was not one to complain. It was the boyishness in him, the deep-down innocence. He scrunched up his nose, rubbed his palms together and looked as if he wanted to play a trick on someone. Then he went through and joined the growing band of clerics, all a little damp, all thawing out with the help of the huge fire that Tourville was busy enhancing.

'The weather's caught us all out,' said Kilgarriff, moving around the room.

'I was ready for it,' said McNutt. 'But I had forgotten just how steep that hill is. I should have tied some chains on the tyres.'

'Yes, it's quite a climb,' Kilgarriff agreed, placing a hand on McNutt's shoulder as he circled. He suggested that everyone move through into the dining room. Tourville was ahead of them to begin uncorking the wine. As soon as the sound of corks popping caught the air, clerical tongues opened out like petals. They looked a lonely bunch, the whole lot of them. Weaving in and out of the little cliques, Tourville poured the wine. Out came the Barolo, with McNutt taking a good dose of the stuff, nodding graciously this way and that. He was not in Cardinal red today. He wore black like the rest of them. And McNutt was warmly greeted by everyone. The cardinal was well liked among the clergy. He took the vine as good as any of them, and could swing his golf clubs as neatly as he swung the thurible when whisking heat into the burning charcoals.

'News?' he asked Kilgarriff. 'How's Harvey getting along?'

Kilgarriff was a little distracted by the Vocations Director, who was filling his left earhole with all sorts of information. How few candidates there were this year; perhaps they might let out seminary rooms to the public; the drop-out rate had improved little this year. Kilgarriff managed to shake him off and turn his attention to McNutt.

'Harvey? News? None at all,' he said. 'Well, hardly any. Just the rubbish the papers print.'

'Yes, of course, but where do you think the dear fellow is? He could be on the street or anything. I'm quite worried about the dear chap.'

Kilgarriff winced at this. McNutt's unwavering compassion for his fellow men got on his nerves. Kilgarriff saw a need for a harder-nosed religion, something from the old days, whatever they were. McNutt was altogether too soft, and Kilgarriff couldn't stand his grubby, down-to-earth love for others. As far as McNutt was concerned, unconditional love and dirty fingers went together. But Kilgarriff didn't want a rag for a soul, he wanted a filing cabinet. Nice, clean, organised, like an audit.

'We don't know what has become of him,' Kilgarriff admitted, knocking back the rest of his wine. 'He could be anywhere by now.'

Fortunately, McNutt had not caught wind of his lies about the Little Sisters of Mercy.

'No Brunello?' asked McNutt, examining the various bottles of wine.

'No. No Brunello.'

McNutt sipped happily at his wine, acknowledging the growing body of priests, canons and Monsignors that had arrived. He made a point of catching the eyes of the newer clergy, settling them in as it were.

'You didn't say if, you know, you think the fellow's mind is affected,' he whispered to Kilgarriff. 'I am very concerned about his well-being. The lid, so to speak, hasn't fallen off the ciborium, has it?'

'I rather think it has,' said Kilgarriff. 'He has been acting out of character, hasn't he, to say the least. I wrote to him, of course, and tried to be sympathetic, offering him a transfer to another parish. We managed to keep the other business quiet. It was a messy affair, wasn't it?'

McNutt nodded sagely.

'We should be able to keep everything hushed up,' Harvey continued. 'We've managed before. We've had to. There was no need to leave like that and draw attention to himself. Now the press are having a sniff, we don't know how much they'll dig up. We must do all we can to keep his weather-house tricks out of the public eye. We might have to open our purse a little wider, who knows. We can do without the bad publicity.'

'What can we do for Harvey?' asked McNutt, not impressed by what Kilgarriff had to say.

'We can only wait. Finding him would prove difficult and solve nothing.'

'Except his distress,' McNutt rebuked him. Then he drew his fingers across his narrow chin, sensing that he had heard enough and that the gathered crowd had become too quiet in their attempt to hear their discussion. He took Kilgarriff by the elbow and led him to the tables of food.

'Let's start them off,' he said.

Kilgarriff agreed, patting McNutt on the back.

'Good idea.'

'And James,' McNutt whispered in his ear, his fingers hovering over the bowl of black olives, the coldness of Kilgarriff's heart not lost upon him, 'let us wait for him with open arms.'

14

Templeford Junction had been good to Crystal. He stole time easily, brought pain and anger to many. But he was restless. Even Molly saw a change in him. His eyes had somehow gone out and jelly took their place. However many fags she laid on his blistered lip, they did not light up properly, barely flickered with life. It was as if Crystal had left his body. A veil fell between him and Molly. She couldn't work out what was the matter with him. He sat next to the newspaper stand on the little wooden stool she kept for quiet moments when there were few people about. He had stopped pacing up and down the platform. Now he just sipped from the strong cup of coffee she had given him, steam dampening his filthy face, weaving between the stalk-like bristles.

'I wish I knew what was wrong with you,' said Molly. 'What's up?' But Crystal wasn't saying. She knew all about his strange need to waste other people's time and saw little harm in it really. She knew he wasn't the sharpest of tools, but that was no reason to reject him. After all, she had met lots of folk more dangerous or weird.

Molly shook her head and moved back into her little kiosk, checking the columns of silver and bronze, cutting the tight nylon bands from a pile of newspapers. One of what she called the big trains had come in, and already the tiled subway echoed with thundering feet. The thundering grew heavier until the neck of the subway haemorrhaged with people. The blur of coats, hats, and rigid little faces intent on getting home joined with hands thrust forward at her kiosk, money pocketed and papers folded and pushed out. Every few seconds Molly shouted: 'Eee Post. Getya Eee Post.' The sudden trade was over in a few minutes.

Crystal's voices had never been so fierce and unrelenting. Filth, shocking filth filled his ears. He had never heard anything like it before. They were getting much worse. They bored down into his skull, screaming and shouting sometimes above the noise of the crowds and trains. The cup of coffee shook in his hands and now and then he had to close his eyes in desperation, let the coffee burn at his lips. Once or twice he shouted out loud to try to drown out the voices, to block them. But they came back worse than ever, louder than ever. Coffee splashed over his legs and down onto the platform. The voices ate his nerves, fed on his terror, his panic.

'That's most of them done,' said Molly, taking another break from her kiosk, rubbing her raw fingers together and drawing two Park Drives from her apron pocket. She handed one to Crystal.

'The voices again?' Molly asked. But Crystal didn't answer. He took the cigarette though, waited for her light, and puffed away. Then suddenly he stopped drawing on it and looked blankly ahead. The cigarette lowered and hung limply from his bottom lip.

'Thanks,' he finally told her. At the edge of the platform a few snowflakes danced in the wind before falling away into the pit where the track ran.

Ash fell in instalments onto Crystal's oilskins and the station grew quiet. There were wet footprints still on the platform and a cleaner moved with a sadness all her own along the empty train that stood at the next platform, a black bin liner in one hand, a rag in the other. Crystal was still on another planet. It was as if he had plugged himself into silence. His eyes just stared ahead. He did not belong to the world. Molly took the little white plastic cup from him and refilled it for herself.

'Too cold for sitting about,' she moaned, wrapping her fingers around the steaming cup. 'Could do with one of those heaters that blows out hot air.' But Molly was speaking with the certain knowledge that Crystal was out of it. Still, she had a habit of talking to herself these days now that her marriage to Eric had broken down. Not that it had been much of a life together. Still, they met up now and again just to see how each other managed. 'Still alive, then,' she would say to him.

Suddenly, Crystal shot up, knocking the stool over, and stared out across the silent, empty platform. Molly placed her coffee on one side and watched. She knew Crystal saw things as well as heard voices.

'What d'ya see?'

Crystal did not answer.

Molly grew frightened at Crystal's blenching face, at the rigidity of his stance, his frozen gaze. She came back out of the kiosk and put her arm over his shoulder, knocking his duffel bag to the side. The cigarette she had given him was almost falling from his mouth. He stood riveted to the spot.

Something was out there in the darkness. She kept at his side and watched with him, wondering what the hell he could see. Whatever it was she was glad she could not picture it. There was nothing for Molly but the ringing, concrete silence and an anticipation of trains soon to arrive. Crystal lost all his colour. Only the dirt acted as a poor make-up.

'What is it?' she asked him again, but he would not say.

There was no way that Crystal was going to stay there and give an explanation. The voices were laughing now. Not the funny voices, smiling voices. These were the loud voices, louder than ever, blasting his skull. He turned and ran, faster and faster, towards the parcel yard and then the ditch where the rails glinted. Molly watched his flight up the stairs. He

moved like a fly once he was out in the open air. He ran
down one street and then the other, across the square and past
St Agatha's. Still the voices tore into him. But it wasn't the
voices that he was trying to escape. The voices were as good
as implanted. No, he was fleeing the Time Wasters.

They were coming, despite his efforts. They were coming
just for the hell of it, the voices warned him. His time-wasting
had been futile. It wouldn't stop them. The voices mocked his
simple faith that wasting other people's time would keep the
Time Wasters at bay. 'Did you really think,' they shrieked,
'that you could do that? No, you fucker. Now you're going to
get it!'

Crystal whined. He had been cruelly tricked. But he had no
time to think about it. On he ran, panting, slipping and sliding,
the snow wet and soft and broken down where feet had trod.
A clear sky lay open. Crystal wished he could fly or fall into it.
He was pinned to the earth. There was no escape. All his
running was doing no good. The Time Wasters read his every
movement and kept track of him. No matter how quickly he
raced and darted into alleys, crossed roads, they were not far
off. But Crystal knew that they would always find him. They
were not hampered like him. They did not have legs.

Up on East Vale, Harvey stood outside the hostel. The front
door was closed. He knocked loudly. He did not want to, but
he had little choice. He did not want to look upon Mrs Angel's
terrible, drooping eyelid, but it was biting cold. With the dark
down early from a cloudless sky, it was freezing. Harvey did
not want to spend much time out of doors, even with his big
black overcoat on. He was shivering already. He could see that
Crystal was not in. There was no light coming from the
window. The only light at the hostel was the one filtering out
from Mrs Angel's elegant room.

The door opened, and there was half of Mrs Angel's face
peering round it. Her eyelid fell in disgust. She shooed at him

like some scraggy cat but Harvey just stood there, hands in pockets, not moving. She repeated her gesture but he kept still, blue eyes staring at her. He was bone cold. He shifted about a little in the snow and looked up again.

'What do you want?' she snapped at him.

'Can I come in a moment?'

Mrs Angel folded her arms.

'Come in? Come in? Do you live here? I think not.'

Harvey bowed his head slightly.

'I was staying with Crystal.'

Mrs Angel looked horrified.

'Were you now? This is the first I've heard of it. Roland knows the rules – no guests. Especially not tramps. We are not a lodging house for the homeless. Now bugger off down to the market square with all the others before I call the police.'

'Fine,' said Harvey, his legs cramping a little. His toes felt numb in the poorly insulated training shoes.

Mrs Angel began to close the door. Harvey blocked it.

'But I've left my stuff upstairs.'

The door opened again.

'If I can just get my things?'

Mrs Angel waited until Harvey stepped away from the door and then, with a chilling smile, slammed it shut. He jerked back and almost fell down in the snow, his hands flailing the air to keep him upright. Frustrated, he walked back to the road and looked up at the dark, curtainless window of Crystal's bedsit. Harvey's fingers were stinging cold. He struggled to close the top button of his coat before crossing the road, flicking his head to free the spikes of damp grey hair that hung down like icicles over his forehead. He would have to wait for Crystal to return. Until then, he would keep himself warm.

As he walked away from the hostel, he thought about Christmas. He knew what it held for him: loneliness. He was completely adrift. All he had was the hope that Montgomery would be there when he hit London; that he would take him in and offer some company. But with the snow blowing in his face, it crossed his mind that it might be best after all just to return to Hickley. Or perhaps visit Kilgarriff at Burnt Green and plead for a quiet little parish somewhere in the backwaters of Southwick Archdiocese. But however desperate the situation, Harvey gave little chance for that particular thought to grow. He spat it out. His belly knotted with the idea of returning with his tail between his legs. How on earth could he look Kilgarriff in the face and ask for help? There was just no way that he could return to that life and make a go of it. The weather house would always be there. It would not go away. Kilgarriff would make sure of that. Harvey was finished.

Harvey headed for the Queens Head. It would be warm there, at least. He imagined it would have a real fire or some radiators underneath the seats. There were a few other places he could warm up in, such as the local chip shop, with its backroom of Formica tables and mismatched chairs, or the late night café, but neither of these felt suitable. Besides, they were much further along the road, and Harvey was feeling the cold. The wind-driven snow had got in through the puckered gaps of his coat, and down under his chin onto his chest. Even his eyelashes had caught several of the tiny hosts. Beneath the drooping head of the pelican, laden with snow and unrecognisable as a bird of any kind, Harvey shuffled. There was a sagging canopy nearby, decorated with Christmas lights. Beneath it, keeping dry and with apple-red cheeks, stood the Salvation Army playing carols. Harvey was glad to see them. Normally he had little time for them. Yet as much as he enjoyed their music, the little knife of a lonely Christmas slipped between his ribs. He had nothing to celebrate. The goose was not getting fat.

Harvey kicked snow from his training shoes at the entrance

to the Queens Head and went into the smoke room. There was little smoking going on in the place. In fact, he nearly had the place to himself. There were just four other people. They didn't look at him. Harvey felt grateful, since he knew he looked like a tramp or someone on social security. He bought a pint of best bitter from a depressed-looking barman and sat all alone in the far corner, which he knew, was where lonely people always chose to sit. There was a roaring fire. But he did not set himself before it like some wet towel. He stayed several feet away and nursed his pint, mumbling to himself. In the end, he nursed another couple of pints before deciding that Crystal might well have returned to the hostel.

Harvey hoped he would have enough time to get his bag and umbrella from the bedsit, say his goodbyes, and catch a late train heading to London. He convinced himself that whatever came of such a journey, little could be worse than staying on in the no-place of East Vale. The comfort and shelter Crystal had offered him had been welcome. But now it was time to go. Harvey felt it deep in his bowels. It was a kind of panicky feeling, a feeling of foreboding. He was being urged to move on. It felt like one of his mother's soft intrusions into his mind from beyond the grave, telling him what to do. He decided that he could not afford to ignore it.

15

Father Macmillan plucked a dark, wiry hair from his nostril and twiddled it between finger and thumb before flicking it onto the floor. At his side the tobacco tin lay open, and in the bowl of his left hand his corncob pipe was smoking away. He had done Evening Mass and hoped for an undisturbed night. The hospital bleep which he usually kept in his jacket pocket lay on top of the gas fire. He stared at it briefly, praying the hospital would not beckon; that lungs kept breathing and hearts pumping. But he guessed that it would go off, sooner of later. It nearly always did when he didn't want to be inter-rupted, and rarely when he urged it to peep at him in order to escape an unwelcome visitor to the presbytery.

Nothing much flickered on the television. It was much too early to put on one of his saucy videos that loosened the knot he felt inside. He liked to watch them late at night before retiring. He took up his pipe again and drew smoke from the moist tobacco, poking at the bowl with his slightly browned finger. His videos were his daily perk. They kept him going. He excused his need to watch ladies of light undressing before him. He was so lonely and needed an outlet. God would understand, he had decided long ago. He always tried not to disgrace himself and let his seed out, but more often than not the desire would be overwhelming, especially if he arranged himself, as it were, right up against the screen. If he held a mirror and went close to his ladies of the light, he could believe that the dots that made up their mouths had really fallen upon him.

As he smoked, glad the bleep kept quiet, he remembered Kilgarriff's demand for him to keep everything hidden. The framed photograph of Harvey still lay on the television as the Archbishop had left it. Harvey's suitcases and boxes remained upstairs, though Macmillan had stacked them out of sight under the bed in the spare bedroom. If he wanted, he could spill the beans. In fact, he had a good mind to after listening to Kilgarriff's lies to his parishioners. Yet he kept his mouth firmly closed. Harvey was getting better, he told his flock. The Little Sisters of Mercy had been doing marvellous work.

Macmillan could see how Kilgarriff trusted him. He had always been the one to keep his head down and get on with it. He never spoke out about anything in all his time as a priest. Over the years he had become a repository for all kinds of hush hush, as he saw it. The weather house wasn't the only secret he kept locked up. There were others. Now and then, when feeling down, when boredom and loneliness filtered into his heart after the ladies of light had performed for him and he for them, he wished he could share these secrets with someone. His pipe had been useful whenever he had felt the urge to do this. The little black stalk would stay on his lip long enough for him to see the shape of the words about to leave his mouth. It would stay against his lip and stop honest words slipping out. He smiled at all the brash comments he had restrained by the simple insertion of his pipe.

Father Macmillan was thinking about his secrets when a shadow fell across the curtains. He sighed hopelessly and got up. He detested visitors at this time of night. He just hoped it was not someone with a marital problem, or another depressed person. Such people always drained him and left him with a restless night. Perhaps it was a request that he give the Last Sacraments. Or maybe it was one of the local tramps, hoping for a late cup of tea and a sandwich. As Macmillan reached the vestibule the doorbell rang.

'Yes, I'm coming,' hissed Macmillan, pushing the pipe further into his mouth before opening the door. He felt like saying, 'Go away and leave me in peace!' With a groan he slid back the three heavy-duty bolts and peered out from the spyhole. The figure standing there was in black. Macmillan could just make out a dog collar. He opened the door.

'Good evening,' Macmillan said, taking the pipe momentarily from his mouth. The fellow priest stared back at him. Not young, not old, perhaps on the threshold of being made a parish priest. He looked cold, rubbing his gloved hands together, and stamping the clinging snow from a pair of overshoes. Macmillan frowned a little but let him into the vestibule without a word. He had never seen this priest before and was quizzical. Then again, Macmillan decided he could have been in the Archdiocese for years. After all, Macmillan kept himself to himself. He hadn't a clue who was where anymore. All that had lost its importance.

'I'm sorry to call on you so late,' said the priest, taking off his gloves and offering Macmillan his hand. 'Richard Buckle – St Mary's on the Mount.'

'Ah, St Mary's, I know it well,' said Macmillan, although he didn't and wondered which part of the diocese that particular church stood in. 'Come in, come in. It's cold in the hallway. Now then, here we are.'

'Thank you? . . .'

'Macmillan. Everyone calls me that.'

'Right, Macmillan. I'm grateful that you opened the door at this time of night. Presbyteries aren't safe anymore. You never know – '

'No, you don't, you're right there.' Macmillan looked steadily at him, puffed on his pipe and then took it from his lip. 'How can I help you?'

At first, Macmillan was going to say that he was just on his way out. But he decided not to be so rude, especially to a colleague. Besides, he rarely had visitors. He took Father Buckle through to the back room and told him to slip out of his coat and make himself at home. The room was cluttered with the remains of Macmillan's television dinner, a tray of collection boxes for Father Hudson's Homes, and a machine for counting coins.

'Could I make a quick call?' Father Buckle asked, looking at the flickering television screen and slipping out of his heavy coat. 'My car's broken down and, well, I was on my way to see my mother. She's not very well.'

'Of course, of course, carry on. It's over there.'

Father Buckle began phoning.

'Do you want me to run you somewhere?'

'That's very kind, but – hello, AA? My car's broken down. Yes, can you help me?'

Macmillan drew greedily on his pipe.

'Yes, I am a member.'

He gave the details of where he had left his car and which way it was facing.

'Away from Hickley,' he told them. 'Yes, that's right, on the main road. How long do you think – gosh, I see. You can't – no, I see, the weather. Oh well, I'll just have to wait. Thank you. Goodbye.'

'Problems?' asked Macmillan.

'They can't give me a time. They said it might be anything up to two hours or more. Everything is snowed up.'

Well, thought Macmillan, the ladies of light will be coming late tonight. Not to worry. Here was some real company at long last. He picked up his tobacco tin and refilled his pipe.

'Oh, I'm sorry,' he said, thumbing the strands into the bowl. 'Can I offer you tea or coffee?'

'Tea would be nice. Could I just phone my mother?'

'Carry on. Would you like something stronger in your tea?'

Father Buckle nodded to him and picked up the receiver. 'That would be great. I'm not putting you out, am I?'

'Not at all, not at all. I'm glad to have some company.'

'Hello, Mother,' said Buckle with the receiver pressed closely against his jaw. 'No, I'm fine. Really, I am. Yes, I'm all right. Yes, I know the roads are treacherous. I'm afraid the car's packed up and I'm going to be late.' A silence followed and then Buckle began again. 'Yes, I've called them out. Don't worry about me, I'm perfectly fine. I'm down at St Patrick's, you know, at Hickley. Listen now, don't wait up. I'll let myself in and I'll see you in the morning. Okay, goodbye.'

He replaced the receiver. Macmillan stood waiting, two mugs of whisky tea in his hands.

'There, that should warm you up. Come over and sit down by the fire.'

'Thanks, you're very kind,' said Father Buckle.

Macmillan took the stalk of pipe from his mouth and began sipping at the tea. Then he looked at his guest a little more closely. He wore a light blue clerical shirt that was more Anglican than Catholic. His dog collar hung a little too loosely in its neck sleeves, as if at any moment it might spring and fall to the floor like a huge toenail clipping. Macmillan couldn't help feeling that there was something awkward about him, perhaps because he kept dabbing at his pock-marked cheeks. He had never seen such red raw craters before. They were deep enough to catch shadows under the lamp. Several glinted with a film of sweat and made them look like little puddles. In fact, Macmillan could imagine snow catching in them during a blizzard, covering the blood red flesh with half-moons. The visitor's head looked a bit like a sieve.

'St Mary's on the Mount,' burst Macmillan, rising from his tea, 'who's there now?'

Buckle sighed and placed his mug on the side table. Macmillan had not detected that St Mary's on the Mount, like the Little Sisters of Mercy, did not exist. He crossed his arms and found a name to give the fool. It was the name of his editor.

'Larkin,' he said. 'Monsignor Larkin.'

'Larkin? Larkin? No.' Macmillan shook his head, puffed his pipe and held it out to his guest. 'I don't remember Larkin. Is he one of ours?'

'He came over with the others from the Anglican Church.'

'Oh, I see, you mean after the – jumping ship like everyone else when they ordained the women.'

'Exactly.'

'Well now, that is interesting. Of course, a great deal of these characters have brought their wives with them. Is he married?'

'Yes, with two children. Two girls. Lovely.'

'And you don't mind?'

'Why should I?'

'Well, of course not. But, you know, don't you feel a bit, well, lonely having a family around?'

Father Buckle wanted to seem authentic.

'It takes some getting used to, that's for sure. How are things with you here?'

'Well, it's great, great. We're out of the smoke here, of course.'

Father Buckle smiled and fidgeted. He seemed to be pondering something. Macmillan drew deeply on his pipe and occasionally looked up at the stranger.

'But you're not out of the limelight, of course,' said Buckle. 'After all, this was Bishop Harvey's parish, was it not?'

Macmillan sighed.

'That was all a sad business,' pressed Buckle. 'It was a big shock to us all. Especially running off like that, after, well, you know after – '

Now Macmillan looked shocked. He shook his head and poked his pipe at his guest. The bleep kept silent.

'You know about all that?'

Father Buckle laughed confidently.

'Good God, yes. It's all over the Archdiocese by now. You know, how he – '

'Dear Lord,' said Macmillan. He stood up and sat back down again and began rubbing his chin. 'His Grace will have a fit. He thinks it is all under wraps, you know, hidden. How much do you know? I mean – ' Here Macmillan thought for a few moments. Obviously, someone had let the cat out of the bag. He suspected Barry Tourville. He had always talked too freely.

'There's no hiding it,' said the visitor. 'What Harvey did will – anyway, there but for the – '

Now Macmillan felt like talking. He thought he was one of the very few people who knew what Harvey had been up to. But now everyone was in on it, it hardly seemed necessary to keep his tongue so tied. He let the smoke swirl in his mouth, filter down into his tastebuds.

'You can never be sure,' he said. 'It's a lesson to all of us. You can never be sure what fills another man's heart.'

'True, very true,' Buckle told him, his finger trailing in and out of the holes in his cheek.

'After all, aren't all men liars? Aren't we born for lies? I think so, you know. When you have a good close look at yourself. When you strip things down and get your fingers in. It's like we're all in the same weather house, you know. We're all in that big weather house.'

'I don't follow you,' said Buckle.

'Ah,' said Macmillan, lifting his pipe into the air. 'You're short on the details, I see. You've only had the trotters. Let me give you the pig.'

16

Breathless, holding his slouch hat to his head, Crystal staggered along Pinckney Road, past the shop and the entrance to the alley. He was burning despite the cold. Water sloshed about in his shorn-off gumboots. His wet long johns clung to his legs. And still the snow whipped stingingly into his face. But the weather was the least of his problems, except, of course, that it made his escape from the Time Wasters all the more difficult.

They were flying over the rooftops of East Vale as he struggled on. He could see them over his shoulder. 'Run,' the voices cried. 'Run, but they will get you. They hate dirty tit-suckers. Do you like sharp teeth? Well, you are going to get them, you fucking bishop-lover. They're going to rip you to shreds!'

Crystal reached the hostel, skidding all over the place, panicking to get his key into the front door. He just about managed, bursting into the hallway and kicking the door shut. He did not see Mrs Angel at her intercom, listening in to her family visitors. He was off up the stairs in bounds, crashing against the stairwell walls, and sweeping away grime with his shoulder.

He raced down the landing and into his room. Once inside, he threw every piece of furniture that he had behind the door like a barricade. The cushionless sofa flew through the air as if it were merely a large sponge. He jammed it at an angle for greater protection. He saw the bare glass window and decided he must cover it up somehow. His fear peaked. The voices grew louder in his head. His skull echoed with obscenity after obscenity. 'The fucking window, window, window,' they howled with maniacal laugher. 'You're going to get it. They're coming to get you.'

In a frenzy, Crystal picked up an old *Evening Post*, the one with the photograph of the bishop and himself at the station. Molly had let him have it for nothing. He put sheets of it against the cold black glass and, using some old Sellotape, secured the makeshift veil. He was desperate to stop the Time Wasters looking in. He could see them now dancing through the sky towards the hostel. Legless, they flew into Pinckney Road. Swarming, they descended over the snow-topped roofs. Crystal jerked away and threw himself heavily on top of the pyramid of furniture. At the window, the two sheets of newspaper hung unevenly, moving in the draught. He chewed the dark bubble on his lip and began to sob like a child. The voices had a field day. They roared all the louder. They mocked him. They drove him madder and madder until he began to howl with them. Beast among beasts, Crystal's throat cracked and gave out a long, chilling wail.

Suddenly, Crystal remembered the mitre that Harvey kept in his holdall. It might protect him from the Time Wasters, he thought, and raced around the room, foot-heavy, looking for it. Bishops are blessed, he convinced himself. They are in God's team. Keep evil at bay. He found the bag, seized the white and gold hat and, throwing his slouch hat to one side, placed it on his head. His head was large and he had to tug it downwards, blanching the skin of his forehead. Then he lay once more against the furnishings, trembling and frightened. 'A fool's hat,' cried the voices. 'That won't stop them. You're a dead bastard now. Watch out! Here they come!'

The invasion began with tapping against the window, which seemed to go on for ages, and then banging at the door. Crystal held on, the gold threads of the mitre glinting under the stark solitary bulb.

Outside, down below, out of sight, Harvey picked up another stone and threw it at the window. He knew Crystal was in, not just because his light was on, but because he had seen him inexplicably hanging newspaper up at the window a few moments before. Perhaps he wanted a little more privacy. A perfectly reasonable explanation, thought Harvey, as he felt for larger stones. He heard a low howling noise coming from inside the hostel. Harvey wondered if it was Crystal. Yet the sound appeared to be coming from the back of the house. Perhaps the nasty Mrs Angel hadn't fed her dog or had left it alone for days on end.

Harvey's aim wasn't particularly good. He had never excelled at sports. Besides, he had had several beers by now, and when he drew back his arm to throw another, he struggled to keep his feet. He let fly again, not too fiercely in case he broke the window, but in a gentle loop. It tapped the glass and fell back down, disappearing into the snow. Still, Crystal didn't answer or signal to him. The howling had stopped. Harvey wondered if Crystal was getting ready to bed down for the night and groaned. He decided to hurl yet another stone, but it missed the window and clicked against the brickwork.

Inside, Mrs Angel was banging her fist against the door to Crystal's bedsit. When she received no answer and tried the door, she found it was locked secure. That made her angry. She didn't allow any of the residents to keep their rooms locked. She only gave them a key to the front door. She slipped off her shoe and began banging the door with the heel. How dare Roland make so much noise when she had her family over, she thought. He will answer to me if it's the last thing I do. Bang, bang, bang she went, each time louder, each time causing her eyelid to close momentarily. She did not care about the noise. Crystal had been making such a racket that a little more wouldn't hurt.

Her family understood. They knew that it was all part of her business. The place brought the money in, of course. Such noise was worth it. After all, she had a glossy black Mercedes on account of the place.

But Mrs Angel was not having any of her residents abusing her authority and breaking hostel rules. She was angry. She had a right to be. And she was going to let Roland know that she was not at all impressed with his behaviour. Not only had he been taking in strangers, but he was also making an awful racket. Her family was a little disturbed by the howling, but Mrs Angel had reassured them that such noise often happened around the time of a full moon. But there was no full moon, her brother had told her. She told him that her residents could feel one a long way off. She would sort things out, she had said. She was the only one now who cared for these people. And she would deal with it. She understood the mad.

Crystal didn't know what to do. The newspaper at the window fell away. The Time Wasters were coming at him from all sides now, tapping at the window with long claws, beating at the door, teeth dribbling. Down below, Harvey could hear distant banging and did not know what to make of it. He looked up at the bright light that now shone from the unveiled window. Almost frozen, his heat stolen by the wind, which had blown up again, driving more snow into the folds of his coat, he cast another stone. This time, with the stiffness and the alcohol, he threw more forcibly and, with a shock, heard it crack the glass. He stepped back, hand to head, and grimaced, hoping Mrs Angel hadn't heard anything. He got ready to run but Mrs Angel did not show at the door.

Harvey looked up at the window and wondered why Crystal did not come to it. He must have heard the noise. If only Crystal would let him in, then he could get his stuff, hand

185

him some money, and go. Moving back into the road, Harvey could see the top half of the room, the bare bulb, but nothing else. His mind told him something was wrong. But he did not move. He stood riveted to the spot.

Crystal stared in horror at the unshielded window and the crack in it. And he saw beyond it, not just his own reflection, ludicrously sporting a mitre, but the Time Wasters like huge moths, rubbing themselves against the glass, bobbing up and down, baring their pointed teeth. Crystal froze. There was nowhere to run. He guessed it would not be long before they burst into the room and devoured him. The voices told him that they would strip him of his flesh. Looking at them, Crystal was in no doubt that they could do just that. He began now to run around the room in a panic, the voices like horseflies, attending his every movement. Crystal was trapped. He was the rat in the corner. He was surrounded. There could be only one way out: the big exit. And as he thought about it, it seemed logical. It would end things. It would take the pain away. He didn't want to die, but he didn't want to live. He ran in a circle, winding up a huge spring of fear.

Harvey did not recognise what fell through the air in a shower of glass and landed with a sickening thud in the snow. When he saw it flying through the air, it was just a rag, a strange, deformed bird. It took days, weeks even, to fall. Harvey's mouth was opening with the slowness of a deep-sea clam. It took an age for the thing to land and begin to bleed. Harvey shook his head. It was all so unreal. Human beings do not look like that when they fly, nor crumple like that when they hit the ground. And it took a long time to recognise that the still body was Crystal. First of all, the oilskins gave it away. Then Harvey stared, perplexed at his mitre lying in the gutter. Then came the face of Mrs Angel, peering down from the glassless window, soon joined by a cluster of other faces. More strange sights followed.

The crumpled figure of Crystal stirred and got up on all fours. Still, everything was in slow motion. Harvey was moving to help him. A patch of snow was dark with blood. This disturbed Harvey as he approached. But, in seconds, Crystal was up and staggering away. Amazingly, he found the strength to walk and eventually break into a loping run, his left foot dragging behind. He made off down Pinckney Road, blood dripping from his wounded leg which had caught the glass as he fell. Harvey looked up at the window for help. Mrs Angel and the others just stared. He shouted at them to call an ambulance and chased after Crystal. He was afraid he would bleed to death. Crystal moved quickly, despite his injury.

Harvey reached the end of the road, puffing for breath, catching sight of Crystal across the tramlines. He was struggling, bumping into the brown shiny tiles of the Fighting Cock before heading off towards Roney Hill. The Salvation Army still played outside the convenience store. Some children were bombing them from above with snowballs scooped up from a window ledge. One caught a tram-wire and broke its snowy back. Another burst against army hats. A third found its way down the tuba. The music carried on with 'Ding-Dong Merrily on High'. It seemed that no one noticed Crystal dripping the occasional bleb of blood. High above the store, the pelican was a strange-looking snowman. It looked all set to fall like Crystal, to hit the ground, crumple, and bleed.

Harvey collided with a couple who had bought a Christmas tree.

'Sorry,' he shouted back as he raced on.

Now he was off past the Fighting Cock, snowballs bursting over his head. There came the laughter of children from high up. Crystal's blood spores were getting more frequent and larger, spreading on the white blotter. But Crystal was out of sight. Harvey got his wind back and continued up the hill. He wasn't used to exerting himself and soon had a stitch in his side. He was jogging more than running, his mouth wide for air, his gold cross and chain bouncing heavily against his ribs. The high shadow of the asylum wall rose to the left. Harvey moved beneath it and into a lull from the wind. What had made Crystal jump? he wondered. What kind of fear could make his crumpled body stand up and run away? And what could Harvey do to help when he finally caught up with him? He just didn't know. But his compassion directed him onwards. He was built to help those who suffered. If there was anything of the priest left in him it was that.

Harvey lost his footing several times, his training shoes gliding away. Each time he reached out to the wall and tried to steady himself. But now and again, he made painful, sprawling genuflections that slowed his progress up the winding hill. Only once did he think of turning back. Go back, he told himself. Just take a train to London. Forget all this. Crystal will survive without you. He is a survivor. Even after throwing himself down from the window, he got back on his feet. But you are not used to such harshness. Get away now, spend Christmas with Montgomery. Mrs Angel has probably called the police by now. Let them deal with it. Crystal is not your problem. Yet compassion came like goose pimples. He could not simply turn around and go the other way. It just wasn't in him.

Behind Harvey lay East Vale, porthole lights from the Three Ships barely visible, and Templeford erased. The whole district, from Hickley Beacon to Metchley, out to Burnt Green and Stonehill, clogged with snow. London too, Harvey guessed, flake on flake. In the blur of white, Harvey felt there was little left to live for: no family; no profession; no love. All snowflakes on the tongue. Here he was, on this strange hill, in a run-down quarter of England, chasing the mad Crystal up towards his former home, Roney Hill Asylum. Now just a demolition site, it was Crystal's only refuge, the memory of asylum.

Harvey could see Crystal, bent forward, slowing down, stumbling into its grounds. What on earth could he hope to find there? he wondered.

Harvey walked quickly, head down, the wind turning against him through the break in the wall. He squinted to mark his path towards where he had seen Crystal disappear, howling wind in his ears, frozen fingers jammed deep into the pockets of his coat. There was nobody around. Roney Hill was deserted. Harvey shouted out for Crystal to stop, but got no answer. Again he tried but the wind stole the words from his lips. On he went, dark trees on either side, the snow luminous, the ground uneven with the remains of the hospital. Harvey called out again. He could just make out the distant figure of Crystal. He appeared to halt, but then carried on, weaving between mounds that were almost all that remained of his old sanctuary.

It occurred to Harvey that Crystal was making his way to the spot where his original ward had stood. He was homing like a pigeon.

'Crystal, stop!' cried Harvey into the wind.

Harvey hurried on, jogging carefully, nearly twisting his ankle.

'Crystal, it's Harvey. Let me help. Wait!'

But Crystal saw what was coming.

Over the leafless trees, through the blinding snowflakes, came the Time Wasters. Swarms of them fell from the sky, jockeying for position. At first, they were hardly noticeable, merely black dots in the murky sky beyond the distant perimeter. But now, Crystal could see the absence of legs, the beating of wings as they moved ever closer, one or two swooping low to the ground, faster and more furious than the others. And the voices were welcoming them in. 'Rip his guts,' they sang. 'Crystal is a dead boy. Eat his fucking head off!' And Crystal heard the wings beating together, flapping like plastic sheeting. He saw them gather and draw near. He began to scream, anticipating terrible pain, closing his eyes for it.

In the wind, with the voices roaring, he knew the first of the beasts would be upon him. In complete terror he opened his eyes, and there was one of them. He kicked out at it. Its coat flaps whipped up in the wind. It came at him again, with blue eyes and glistening teeth. It had a human face, but no legs.

Crystal punched and kicked the thing. He heard it cry out in pain. 'You're dead meat,' the voices raged on. 'Here come the teeth. Here come the teeth. Bite the bastard in half! Chew him up!' Crystal was kicking and lashing out for all he was worth. He saw white teeth blur in slow motion. He felt mad. He saw blood. He heard wings beating. He had the beast by the neck, squeezing it till his knuckles blanched. There was something golden hung around its neck. It was a thick elaborate chain and cross. Crystal wrapped it around his fist and jerked it tight, the beast sinking to the ground.

17

Barry Tourville was up early on Christmas Day. Early enough to catch Kilgarriff in the kitchen, making final adjustments before setting out on his morning run. Even on Christmas Day Kilgarriff was going to prove to himself that he was too young, too fit to go into a box. Fit as a fiddle. Tourville shook his sleepful head and scratched his high, pale brow.

Kilgarriff did not acknowledge Tourville's presence. He was busy pulling on a pair of thick, woollen socks over his training shoes. He did not see his secretary's mystified expression. With a grunt, and a pinch of his bottom lip, he had the socks over the heels and ruckled about his ankles. Standing up, he walked about the kitchen in them, occasionally jumping up and down.

'Why the socks?' asked Tourville.

'To stop me slipping over in the snow.' Kilgarriff beamed a self-satisfied smile, feeling a bit of a genius about his idea. He checked his freshly dyed hair in the mirror. As always, he was pleased with its bogus youthfulness.

Tourville shrugged and made coffee.

'Which route are you taking today?' he asked, not really interested but making an effort since it was Christmas Day after all. Beyond the wet windows, the snow broke up the dark.

'Four, I think,' Kilgarriff told him. 'Down into Burnt Green and up again. The socks should help me do a good time, despite the snow.'

'Hmm,' mumbled Tourville watching steam lifting from his coffee cup.

Normally, Rose would have been in the kitchen, making them breakfast and drinks. But for the first time in years, she had requested time off to go down with Mildred to her sister's house. Tourville thought Rose was still smarting from being left out of the Cardinal's visit. Perhaps she had gone to her sister's on purpose, to get her own back, let them cook their own festive meal.

'So why are you up so early?' asked Kilgarriff, his hair contrasting with the snow outside.

'No reason.'

'Christmas excitement? The reflex of a child?'

Tourville laughed cough-like, and gave his cynical face.

'I don't think so,' he said.

Kilgarriff was jogging lightly on the spot.

'You don't fancy joining me? Open those wind sacs?'

'No thank you. Fitness kills.'

Kilgarriff said nothing, opened the back door, and tested his footwear briefly before jogging round to the front of the house and along the driveway. He had meant to say Merry Christmas to Tourville, but had forgotten. He would say it, he decided, when he returned. As he moved beneath the tree, the intruder light lit up a circle of snow, making him blink. For a second or two, he was just a bright blue tracksuit, then a shadowy thing crunching through the darkness. Already his socks were soggy. The toe-ends flapped about and made him look like some ridiculous elf rushing to hide from the break of day, a trail of prints left to mystify those who chanced upon them.

Soon enough, Kilgarriff was on the hill, looking out over Burnt Green, daubed with a fresh fall of snow. There was his dominion, the Archdiocese of Southwick. He jogged on, steadily at first. Harvey filled his mind. How Kilgarriff wished that even in this, the happiest of seasons, he would come crawling back. He could have wished for no better present than to see Harvey crawling back on his belly. He imagined him, even now, making his way up the hill to Archbishop's House, head down, dejected, no more spirit in him than in a dog. He could see his blue eyes, dull pebbles, and grey hair like some torture device gripping his scalp. And Kilgarriff descending, descending with the widest smile and coldest heart. Descending like a plane. Not like a servant. Not like a friend.

18

Montgomery had read the *Evening Post* and still found it difficult to believe his eyes. He drew close to the two girls, lying naked on the bed, and, kneeling between them, bent forward and bit the skin at the back of the dark-haired girl's neck. Joylyn tensed up, releasing a little burst of air from her wide nostrils. Samantha lay next to her, in the gold wig that Montgomery had bought her. It glittered as she turned her head and reached out with black fingernails to draw Montgomery down on her. But he resisted, sitting back on his heels, shaking his head, still finding it difficult to come to terms with what he had read. He had the paper in his hands. Samantha pouted, gave a sad little schoolgirl face. There were blotches all over her pale flesh, where Montgomery had rubbed his bristled chin.

'You wouldn't have thought he had it in him. Not in a million years,' he said gleefully, fingering his dark mop of matted hair. Samantha laid her head on his scrawny thighs. 'It must have all built up in him, ready to burst, like a greyhound out of a trap.'

Joylyn lit one of the cigarettes she had stolen from her mother. She gave one to Samantha. It landed on her taut belly and rolled between her legs. Samantha laughed and retrieved it. The girls lit up together and blew smoke trails into Montgomery's face.

'He was so bloody English,' Montgomery complained. 'Boring, predictable, a bloody hermit. To be honest, I couldn't stand the guy. He didn't look like he had one good fuck in him. Jesus, what a hypocrite. I can't believe it.'

'Yeah, well, you lot are all funny, if you ask me,' knifed Samantha, with a swish of her wig. 'What do you expect if you fall for that celery crap?'

'Celibacy,' Joylyn corrected her.

'Yeah, whatever. Look at all that stuff you had us doing. Dressing up in those – '

'Cassocks,' Joylyn helped.

'Yeah, and with those candles. I mean, you know, it's – '

Samantha stopped and smoked long and deep, knocking her ash onto the bedsheet. Montgomery got off the bed and walked over to the window of his large flat.

'I hope he doesn't look me up,' he complained. 'I've got this awful feeling that I made the mistake of telling him that if he ever needed help, just get in touch. God, I feel it in my bones, the bugger's on his way here.'

'Yeah? Well, it might be fun,' said Samantha, 'if that story's anything to go by.'

Montgomery scratched his chest, rolled his shoulders, and while folk moved sluggishly along the street below, he opened out the *Evening Post* and read the story over and over.

Despite the lies told by Archbishop Kilgarriff that runaway Bishop Harvey was convalescing with the Little Sisters of Mercy – the order no longer exists – the *Evening Post* has unearthed the truth. Bishop Harvey had turned the presbytery at St Patrick's Church in Hickley into a kind of weather house. We found that the ingenious bishop had knocked a hole through his bedroom wall into the adjacent home of his lover, Olwyn Jones. To the eyes of everyone, nothing was going on between them. They came out of their respective front doors. Outside, they did not speak to one another. Only when they returned to their weather house did the sparks of passion fly. When the truth came out, the Catholic Church was keen to keep the matter hidden and the fledgling bishop went on the run. Archbishop Kilgarriff has declined to comment further on the matter.

19

Cardinal McNutt leaned against a gravestone, the wind slicing through the canopy of trees and against his bowed head. Behind, in the valley, lay Ardinweald, where Harvey was born. It was Sunday. Everything was quiet. Occasionally, midst the hiss of wind-rustled branches came the cry of bramblings jittering in and out of the hedgerow, their rumps like flakes of snow. McNutt watched them fly into the orchard, past the observatory ruins, and land beside the enormous crucifix, rotten, swollen and black. This is Harvey's home now, he thought, looking down at the open grave. He slumped forward, his hands like dead fish, cheeks marmoreal. His small, curving back shuddered and fell still.

McNutt was not alone. Across the wide gravel path, Danny, the gravedigger, sat on a headless angel, waiting to fill the hole in, his clay trousers watery, a cigarette burning close to his thick lips. He was well known in Ardinweald. Not only was he an alcoholic, but the story went that he often shot racing pigeons released from the park below and kept their rings in a jar. McNutt, however, saw no ill will in his kindly, blue-cheeked face. He watched him now, taking the cigarette from his mouth and casting it away. It glowed beneath the huge, swirling sky and dropped into a puddle near his feet.

'I'll have to give them up,' said Danny, noting McNutt's gaze. 'They'll kill me, I know it.' He held out a nicotined finger. 'Look at that!' he said. 'That's me lungs inside out.'

197

Or your liver, thought McNutt, nodding civilly. Danny inspected his fingers and began to bite them clean. It was a fruitless task.

The tombstone next to the open grave was colder than the air. McNutt's hand lay flatly on it, wrinkled at the wrist. The sky was bloating and rubbing itself against the beech trees. McNutt closed his eyes and felt the rain hitting him; big droplets stored up by the dark branches let go in the wind and dribbled down his neck. He wanted to stay beside the maw of earth like an angel, a guardian over Harvey's grave. A feeling of emptiness, hollowness washed over him. For a moment, he thought he enjoyed the feeling, but it was only a trick of his brain. In truth, he had been devastated by Harvey's tragic death. Like Billy in Java, yet another young life taken. And despite all his inconsistency, McNutt saw in Harvey someone who really did love others. Not just playing at it. A real lover of men and women. A gorgeous fellow.

By now, Danny was coughing old smoke from his lungs and spitting phlegm onto the red mud. Or was he merely hinting how both of them were getting very wet? Either way, McNutt was deaf to the rattling of Danny's throat. Down in Ardinweald the sodium lamps came on, glowing strangely pink above the glossy tarmac.

Water ran off McNutt's coat, falling away onto the pale green spikes of grass. The funeral party had long gone. There had been a small crowd, all wearing dreadfully shocked faces, whether shocked or not, carrying words like salt on their tongues. Archbishop Kilgarriff, aspergillum in hand, had sprinkled holy water at the deep hole. His lack of sincerity in his graveside address was not lost on McNutt, who had already decided that the Archbishop should never have a cardinal's hat in his wardrobe.

'I'll have to − finish things now,' said Danny suddenly, his voice deep and persuasive.

'Things?' McNutt looked up, a few tears mingling with the rainwater.

'The grave, Your Eminence. Before the rain gets any heavier.' Danny was right. McNutt wiped his face and looked at the sky. It was difficult to distinguish where the sky ended and trees began.

'A moment more?' he asked heavily.

'Okay,' said Danny warmly, his foot resting on his spade which he carried everywhere with him.

McNutt smiled briefly and closed his eyes again. Danny, resigned to a longer wait and noting a break in the rain, rooted in his pocket for his cigarettes and lit up. Down in the valley the sodium lamps slowly turned bright orange. The observatory ruins darkened against the lilac horizon. Danny blew his smoke in the direction of the Sow's Ear.

McNutt bowed his head, crossed himself and moved away from the grave. Danny was glad he was going now. He was missing valuable drinking time. He flicked his cigarette away and swung himself upright. Without warning the rain grew heavy again. It struck maliciously, whipped up by the wind, driving through the cobweb of branches onto the pair of them. As each drop hit the ground it exploded into a silver tree of water.

'I'm sorry I kept you,' McNutt apologised, having ended his silent vigil.

Danny waved his hand into the curtain of rain.

'No problem whatsoever,' he told him, walking away from the headless angel. 'I'll walk with you to the gate.' He lifted his spade onto his shoulder. 'It was an awful thing, Your Eminence. A great shock. To murder a bishop!'

The rain ceased suddenly. They walked along the path towards the crucifix and the large wrought-iron gates, the gravel crunching beneath their feet. A brambling flew past, crying chucc-chucc-chucc as it went.

McNutt imagined he heard Harvey's voice crying out through the mud. He blocked his mind as best he could and looked into the shrubbery at the side of the drive. He thought he caught sight of a fox. Beyond the iron railings, something skittered away through the wet grass.

As they reached the end of the drive, he looked at Danny's heavy spade. He noticed how his fingers were chapped and thick, uncut nails filled with dirt.

'It must be hard doing what you do,' he said.

'Oh, devil hard sometimes.'

'With all that digging.'

Danny put his spade on the other shoulder.

'I'm up and down like a whore's – ' He stopped, froze, realised that he was not in the Sow's Ear yet. 'I'm sorry, it's what we – ' He fell silent and walked on without another word.

When they reached the end of the drive, Danny bid the Cardinal farewell, and set off back towards the grave to fill it in. McNutt looked up. One of the sodium lamps hadn't changed to orange. It hung like a pomegranate seed above the miserable, oily, deserted pavement. He moved beneath it, his head sore from the cold, thinking only of Harvey.

20

Olwyn looked down the half-submerged steps of Tenby Harbour. No one was with her. She had left her mother in the kitchen, cooking their dinner. Her mother did not see the newspaper fall from her daughter's hands, nor the dreadful look on her face. Nor did she hear Olwyn leave the flat, go downstairs, walk numbly between the rows of pottery, past the new gorse bush perfume that Brother Anselm had supplied. Olwyn was careful not to make a sound, reaching up to stop the bell above the shop door from sounding as she made her exit.

She walked down to the harbour, passing the little kiosk where her father had sold his fishing trips. A different company name now adorned the blue wooden slats, and a blackboard awaited the scribbled list of sailing times during the holiday season. But now the whole town had that silent, deserted look. Rust was showing. Repairs had not yet been made to properties. High above, the pastel-coloured hotels and guest houses were shedding skins of rare snow, and looking in need of a lick of paint. Even the back of her shop, Pottery & Pieces, looked forlorn.

Olwyn kept her eyes fixed on the spot she had seen Harvey all that short time ago, clambering out of the Caldey boat at the end of his retreat. Now, no boat rocked against the harbour wall. No half-moon black tyres against the worn stone, or boys throwing ropes. No Harvey lifting himself over the gunwale.

WITHDRAWN